Enid Blyton

THE FAMOUS FIVE
FIVE GO ADVENTURING AGAIN

THE GRAPHIC NOVEL
By Béja and Nataël

HODDER CHILDREN'S BOOKS

First published in Great Britain in 1943 by Hodder & Stoughton Limited
Graphic novel adaptation first published in France by Hachette Livre in 2018
and in this format in 2020
This edition published in 2022 by Hodder & Stoughton

1 3 5 7 9 10 8 6 4 2

nd Enid Blyton's signature are
er & Stoughton Limited
) Hachette Livre, 2020,
K Salinas © Hachette Livre, 2020
r & Stoughton Limited, 2022
ing by Rachel Ledrich

A CIP catalogue record for this book is available from the British Library.

ISBN 978 1 444 96368 7

Printed and bound in China

The paper and board used in this book are made from wood from responsible sources.

Hodder Children's Books
An imprint of
Hachette Children's Group
Part of Hodder & Stoughton
Carmelite House
50 Victoria Embankment
London EC4Y 0DZ

An Hachette UK Company
www.hachette.co.uk
www.hachettechildrens.co.uk

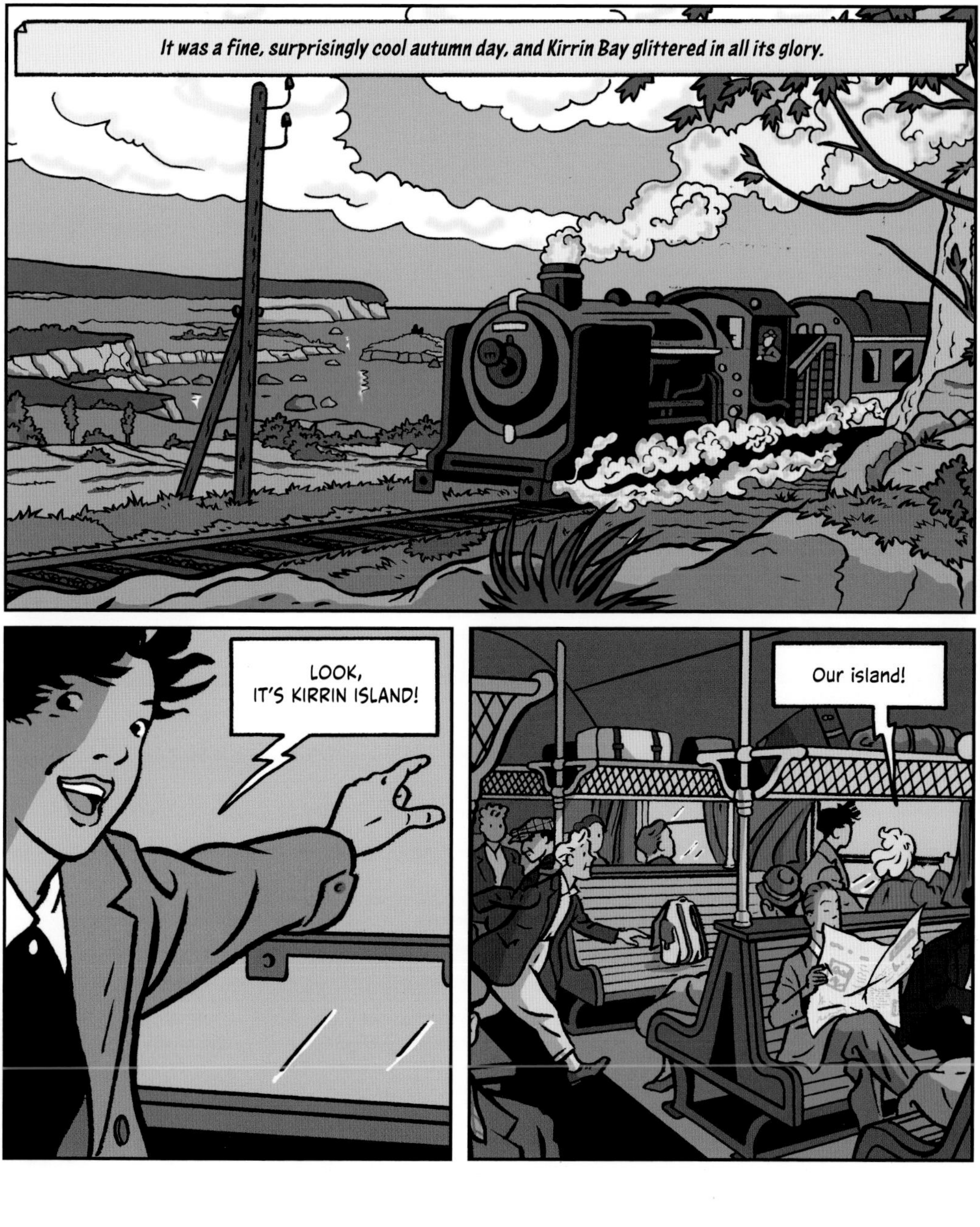
It was a fine, surprisingly cool autumn day, and Kirrin Bay glittered in all its glory.
LOOK, IT'S KIRRIN ISLAND!
Our island!

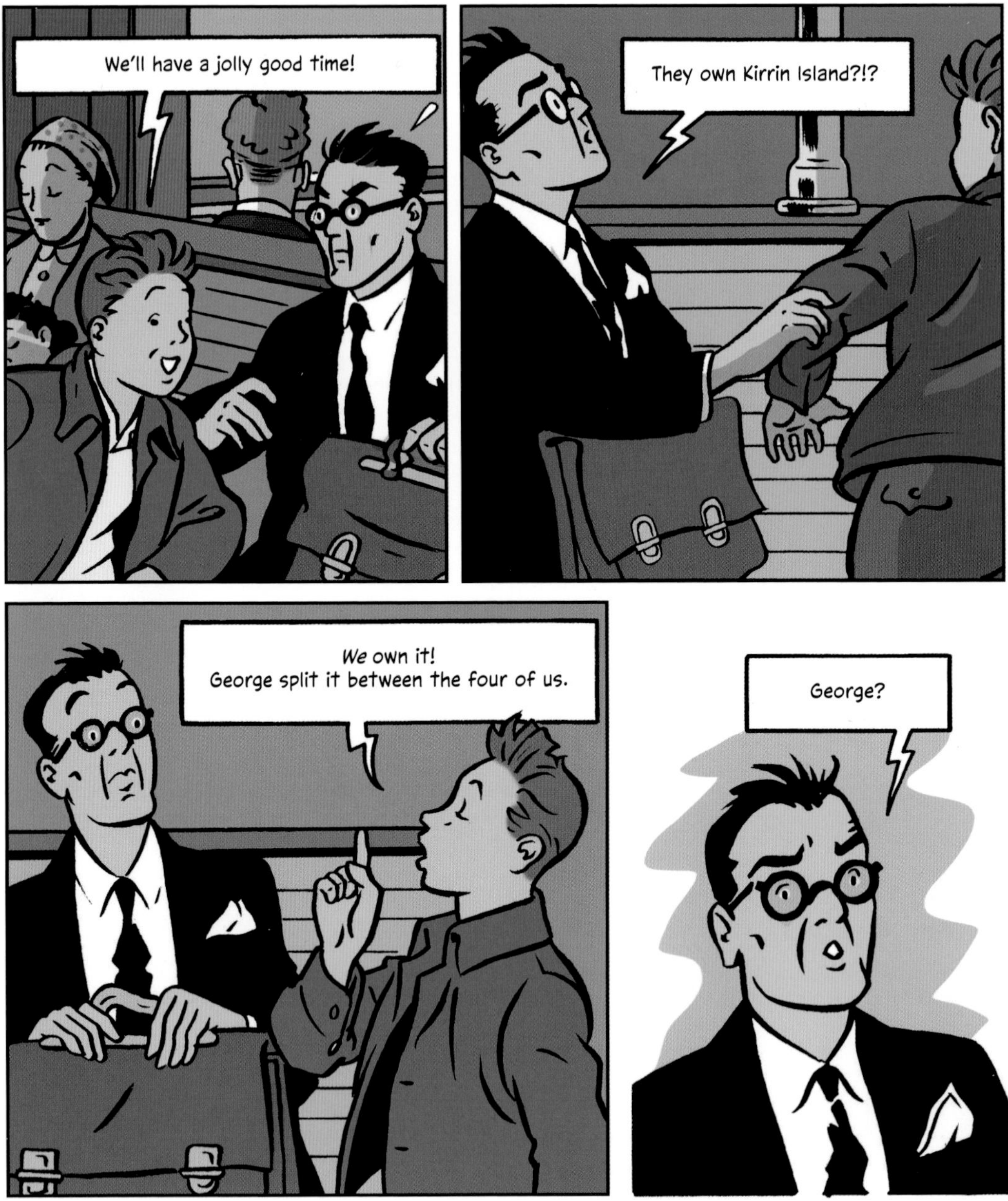
We'll have a jolly good time!
They own Kirrin Island?!?
We own it! George split it between the four of us.
George?

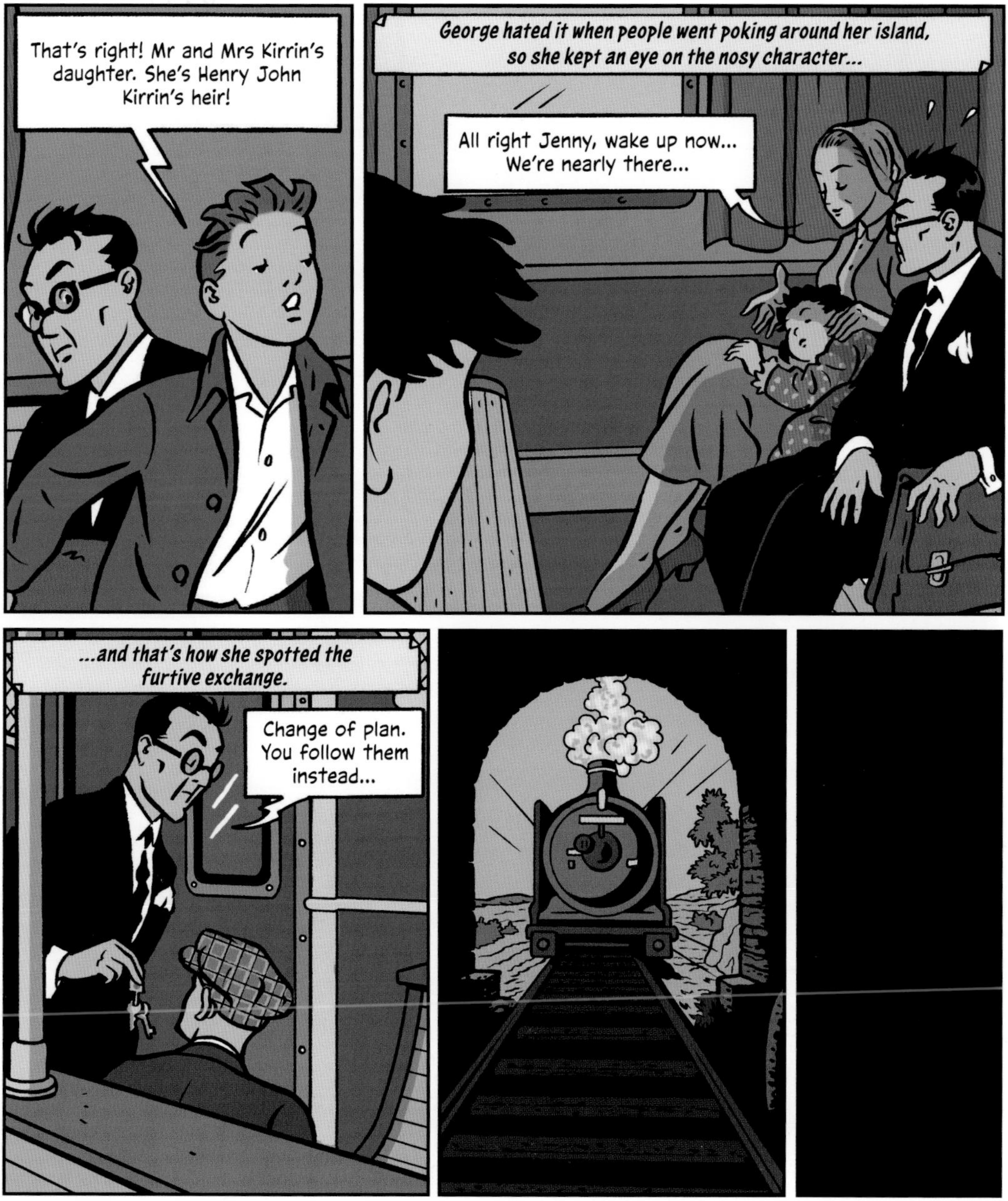
That's right! Mr and Mrs Kirrin's daughter. She's Henry John Kirrin's heir!
George hated it when people went poking around her island, so she kept an eye on the nosy character...
All right Jenny, wake up now... We're nearly there...
...and that's how she spotted the furtive exchange.
Change of plan. You follow them instead...

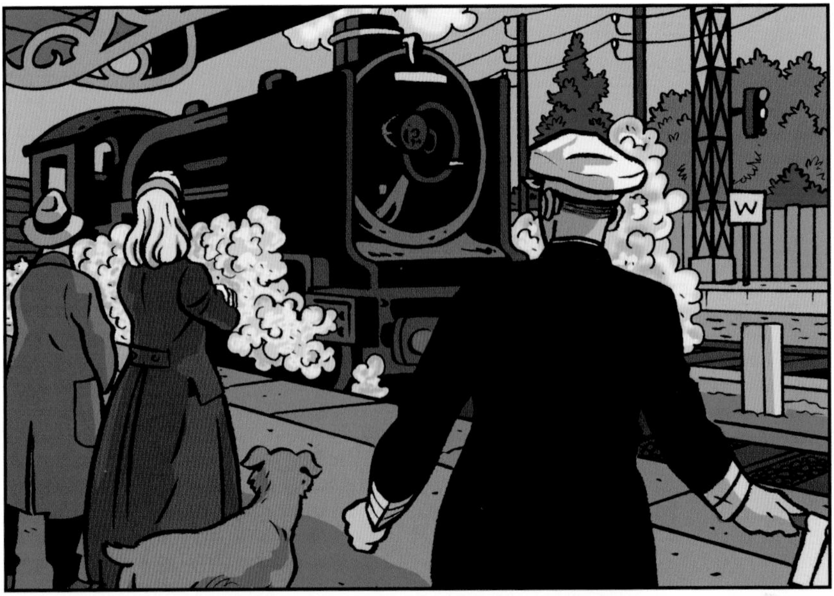

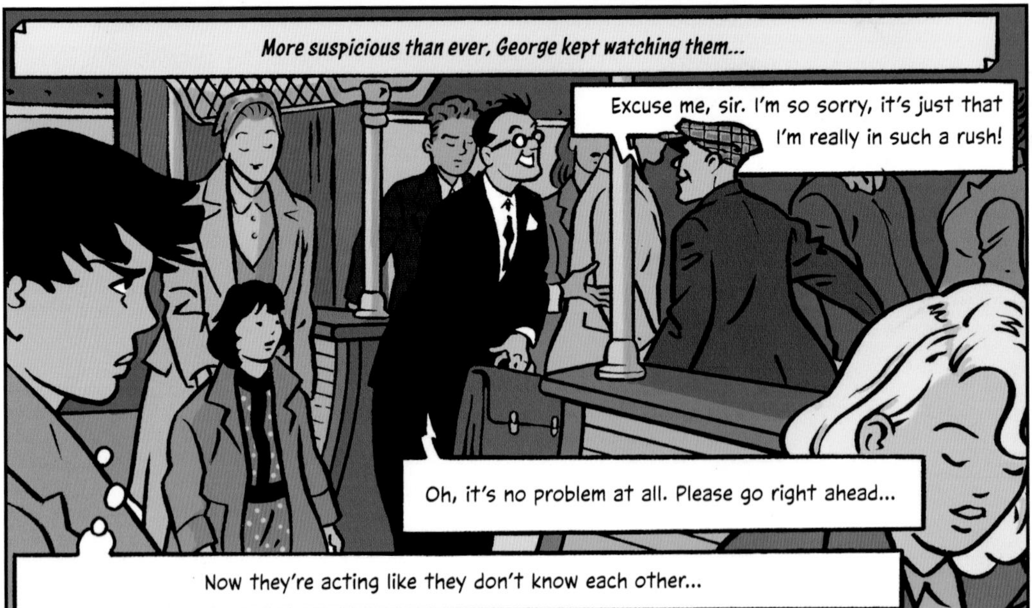
More suspicious than ever, George kept watching them...
Excuse me, sir. I'm so sorry, it's just that I'm really in such a rush!
Oh, it's no problem at all. Please go right ahead...
Now they're acting like they don't know each other...

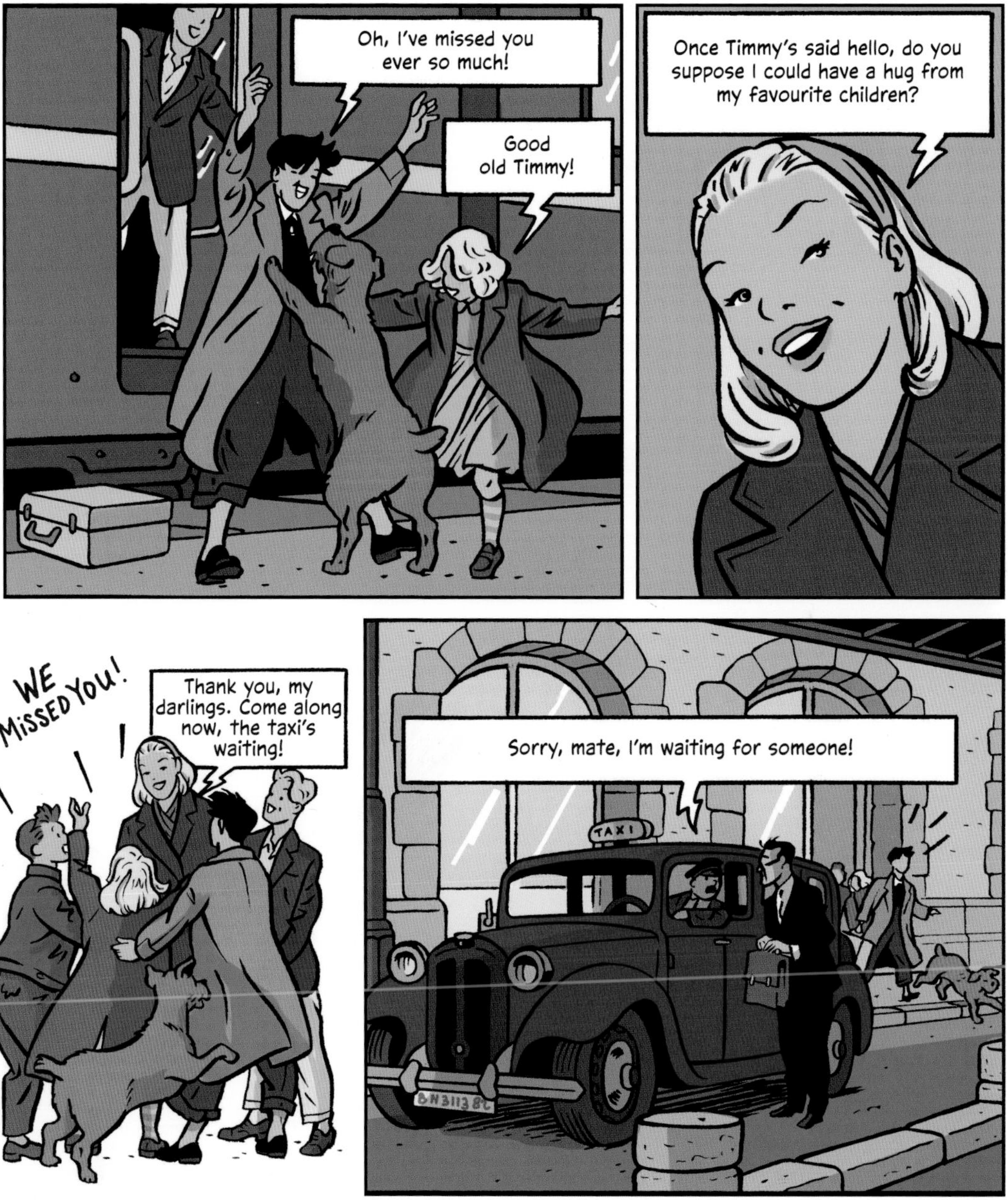
Oh, I've missed you ever so much!
Good old Timmy!
Once Timmy's said hello, do you suppose I could have a hug from my favourite children?
WE MISSED YOU!
Thank you, my darlings. Come along now, the taxi's waiting!
Sorry, mate, I'm waiting for someone!
TAXI

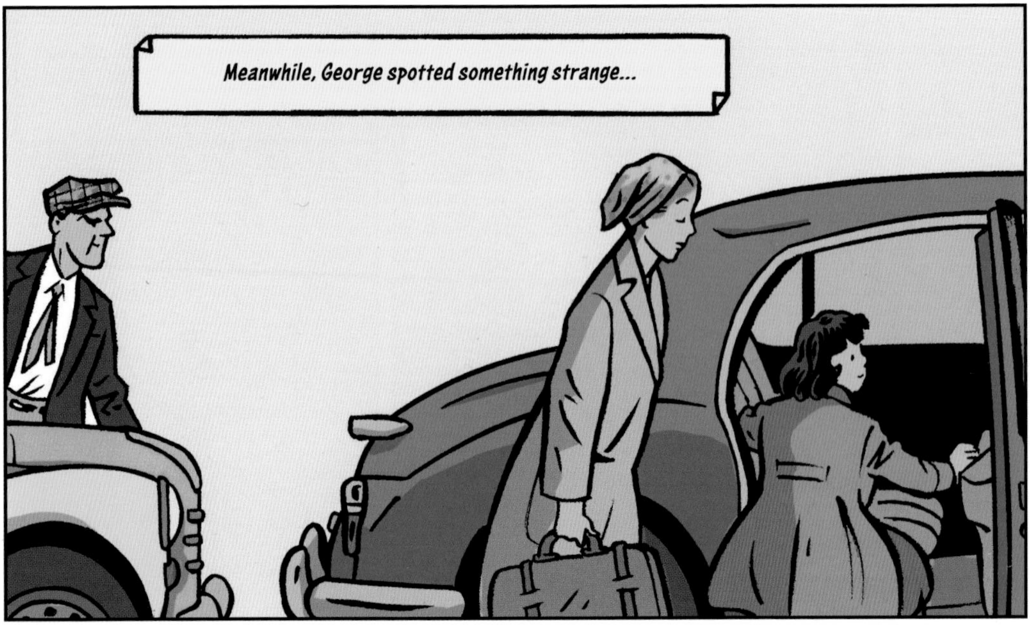
Meanwhile, George spotted something strange...

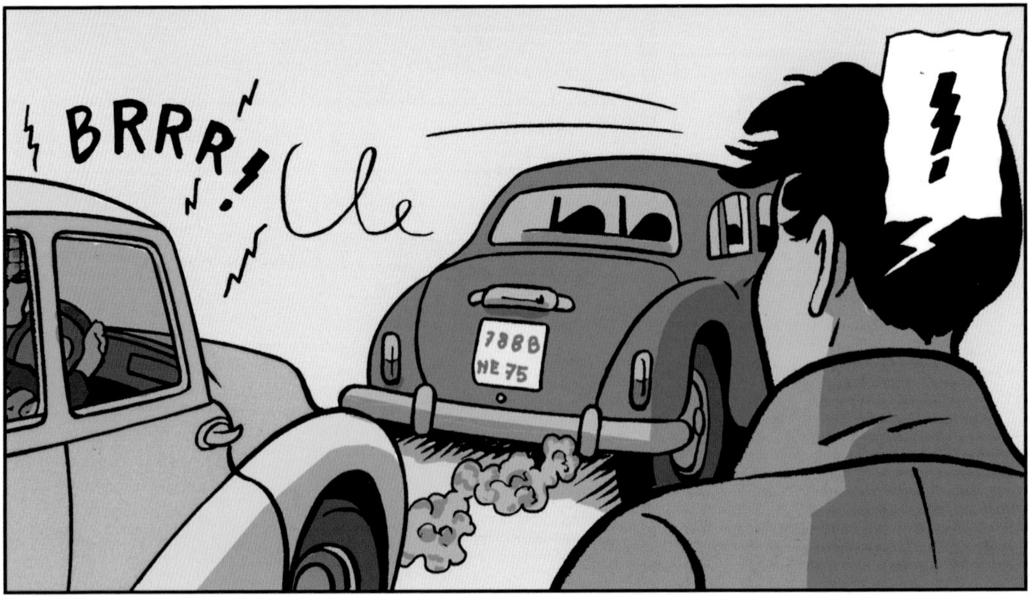
BRRR!
7888
NE 75
!

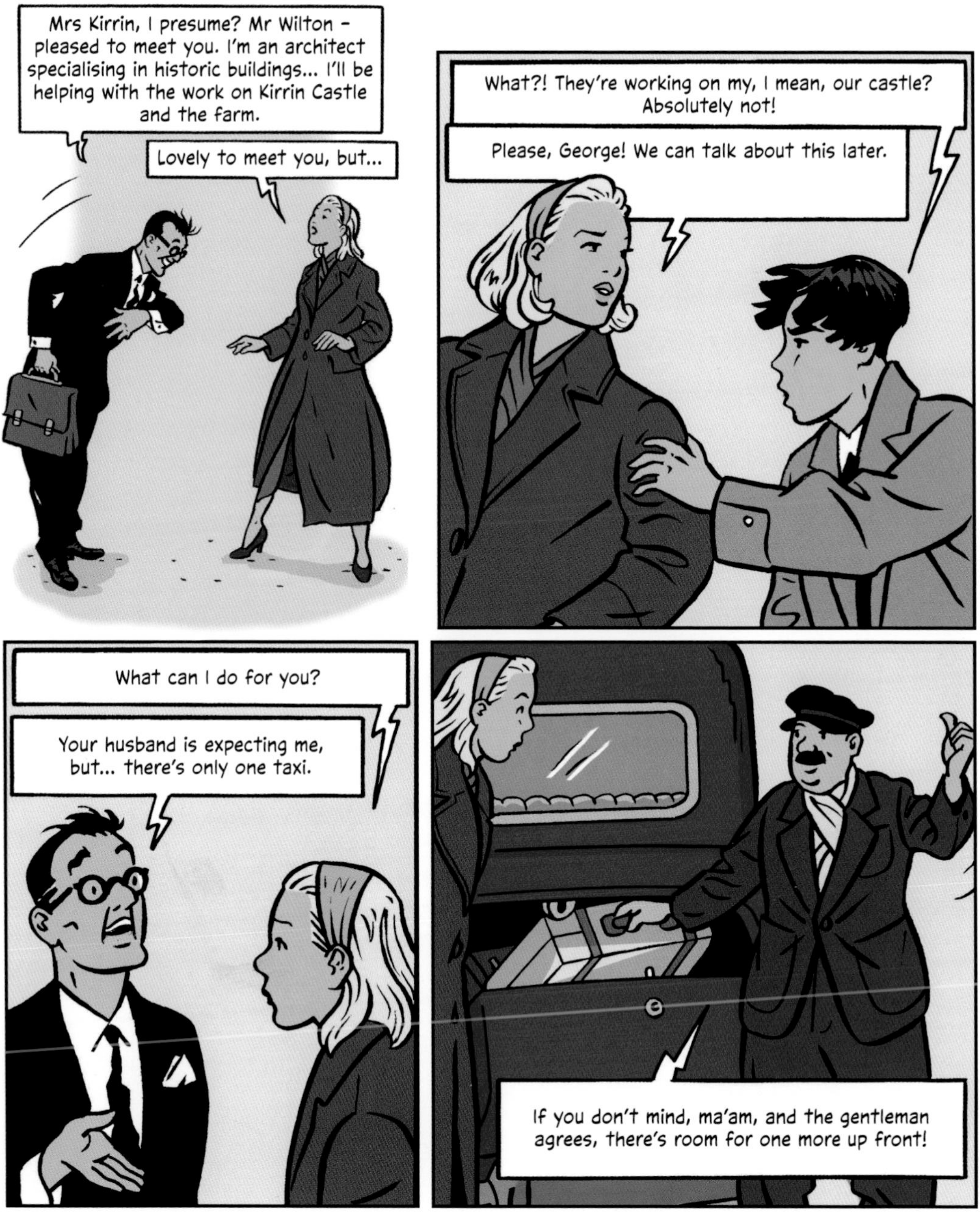
Mrs Kirrin, I presume? Mr Wilton – pleased to meet you. I'm an architect specialising in historic buildings... I'll be helping with the work on Kirrin Castle and the farm.
Lovely to meet you, but...
What?! They're working on my, I mean, our castle? Absolutely not!
Please, George! We can talk about this later.
What can I do for you?
Your husband is expecting me, but... there's only one taxi.
If you don't mind, ma'am, and the gentleman agrees, there's room for one more up front!

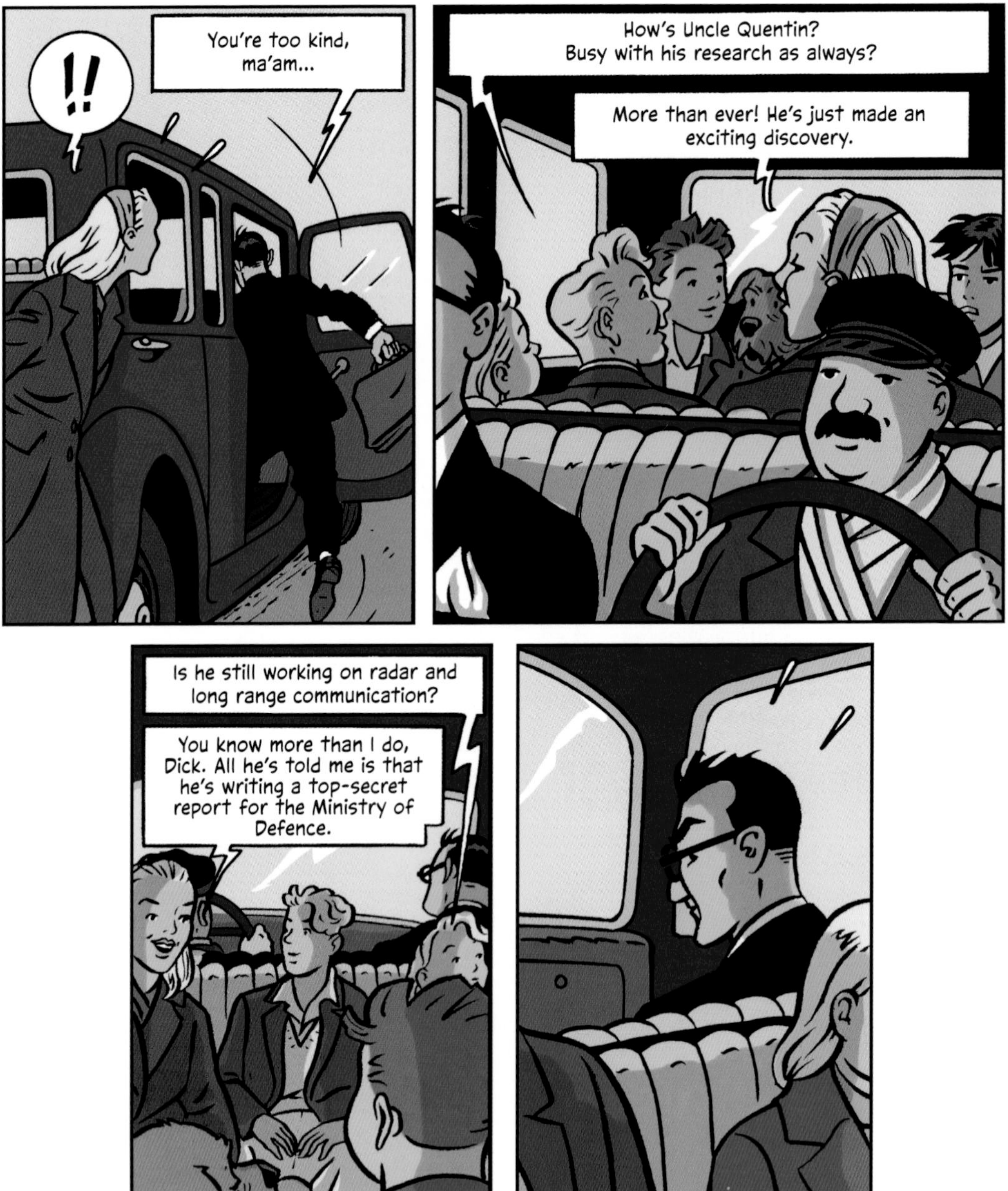
!!
You're too kind, ma'am...
How's Uncle Quentin? Busy with his research as always?
More than ever! He's just made an exciting discovery.
Is he still working on radar and long range communication?
You know more than I do, Dick. All he's told me is that he's writing a top-secret report for the Ministry of Defence.

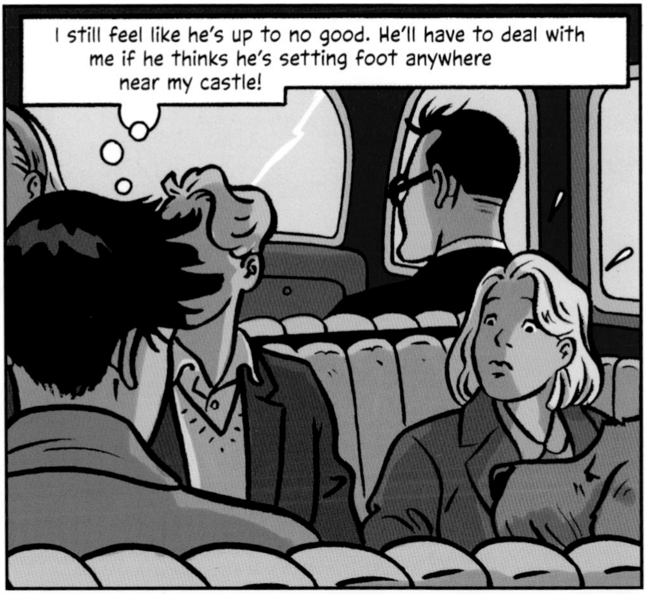
I still feel like he's up to no good. He'll have to deal with me if he thinks he's setting foot anywhere near my castle!

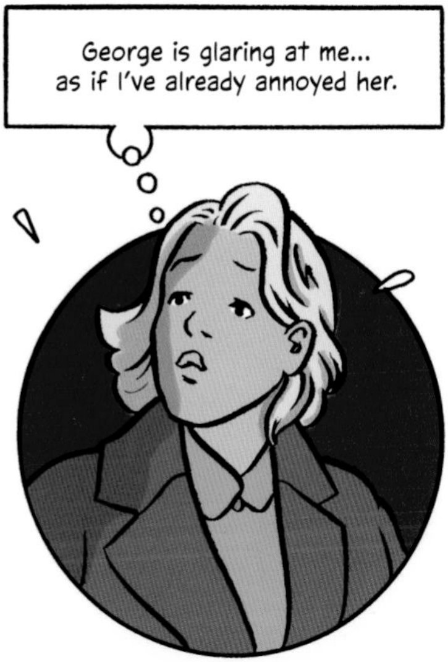
George is glaring at me... as if I've already annoyed her.

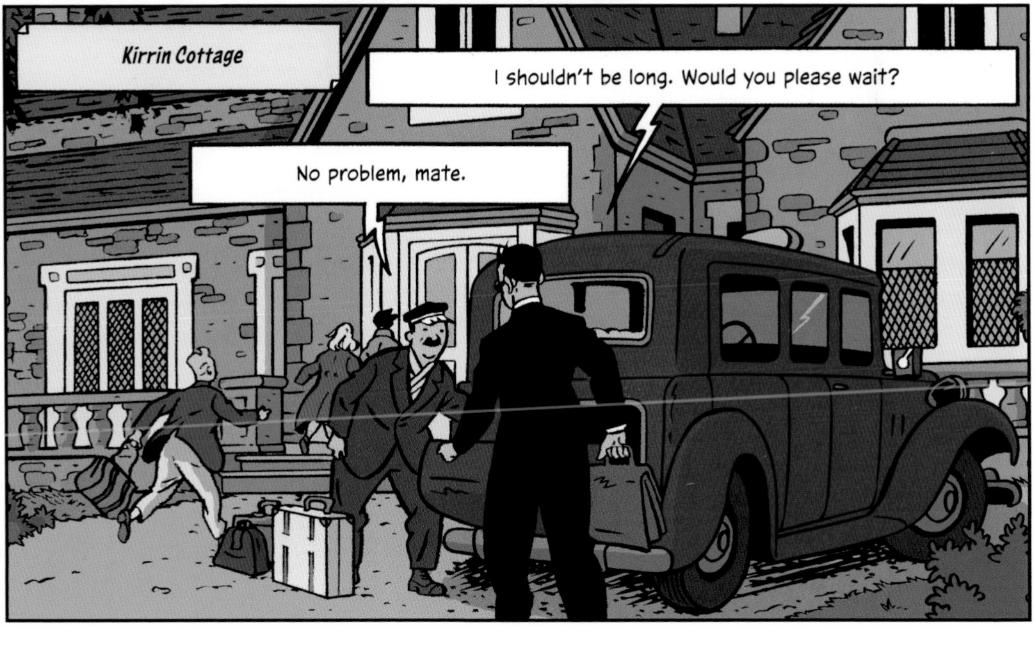
Kirrin Cottage
I shouldn't be long. Would you please wait?
No problem, mate.

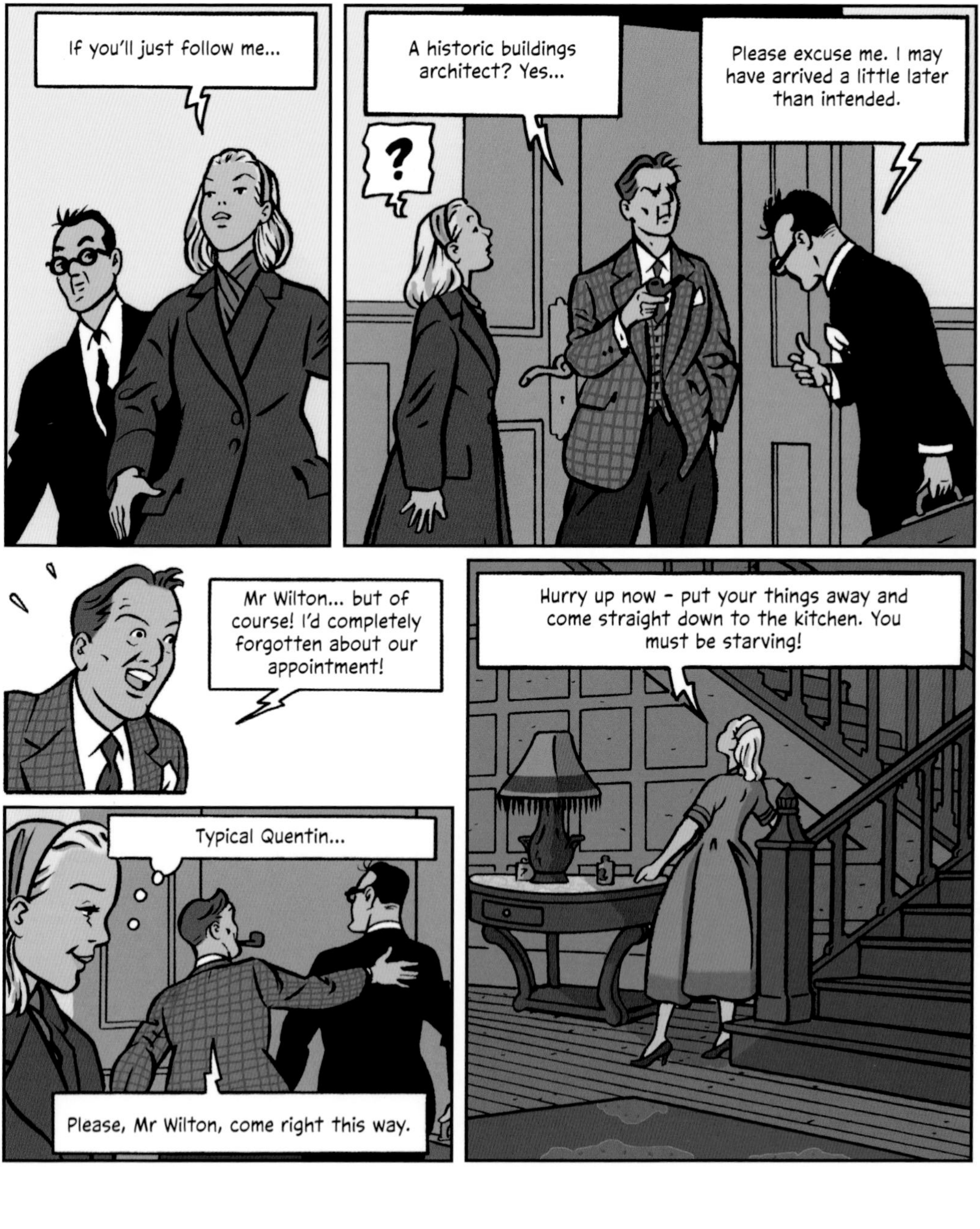
If you'll just follow me...
A historic buildings architect? Yes...
?
Please excuse me. I may have arrived a little later than intended.
Mr Wilton... but of course! I'd completely forgotten about our appointment!
Typical Quentin...
Please, Mr Wilton, come right this way.
Hurry up now - put your things away and come straight down to the kitchen. You must be starving!

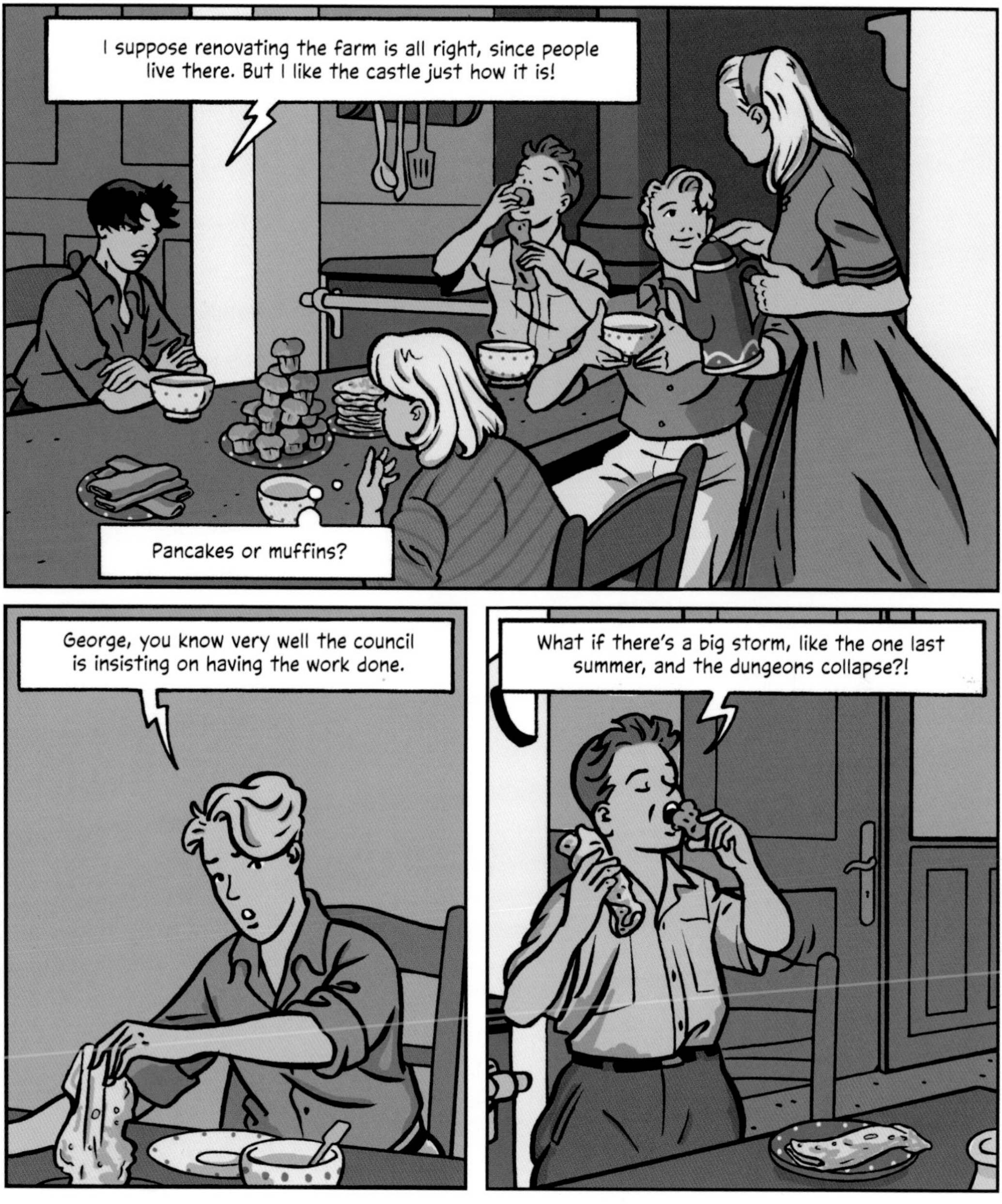
I suppose renovating the farm is all right, since people live there. But I like the castle just how it is!
Pancakes or muffins?
George, you know very well the council is insisting on having the work done.
What if there's a big storm, like the one last summer, and the dungeons collapse?!

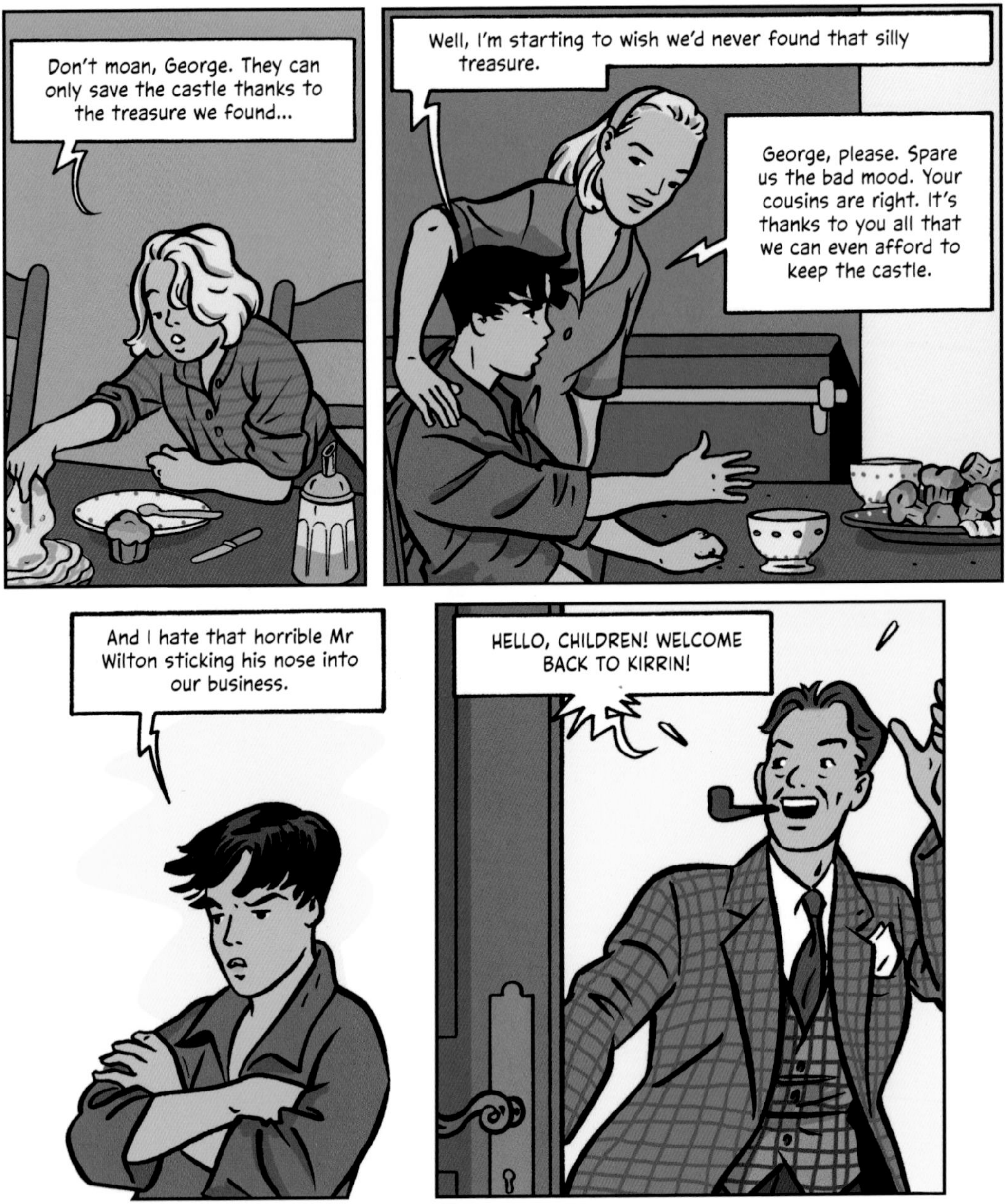
Don't moan, George. They can only save the castle thanks to the treasure we found...
Well, I'm starting to wish we'd never found that silly treasure.
George, please. Spare us the bad mood. Your cousins are right. It's thanks to you all that we can even afford to keep the castle.
And I hate that horrible Mr Wilton sticking his nose into our business.
HELLO, CHILDREN! WELCOME BACK TO KIRRIN!

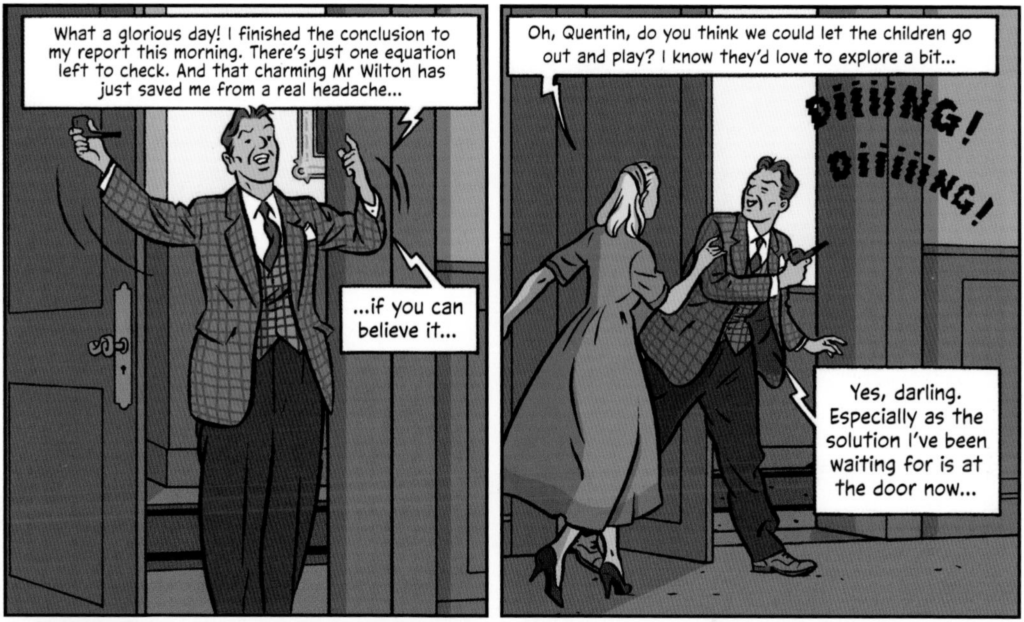
What a glorious day! I finished the conclusion to my report this morning. There's just one equation left to check. And that charming Mr Wilton has just saved me from a real headache...
...if you can believe it...
Oh, Quentin, do you think we could let the children go out and play? I know they'd love to explore a bit...
DIIIING! DIIIIING!
Yes, darling. Especially as the solution I've been waiting for is at the door now...

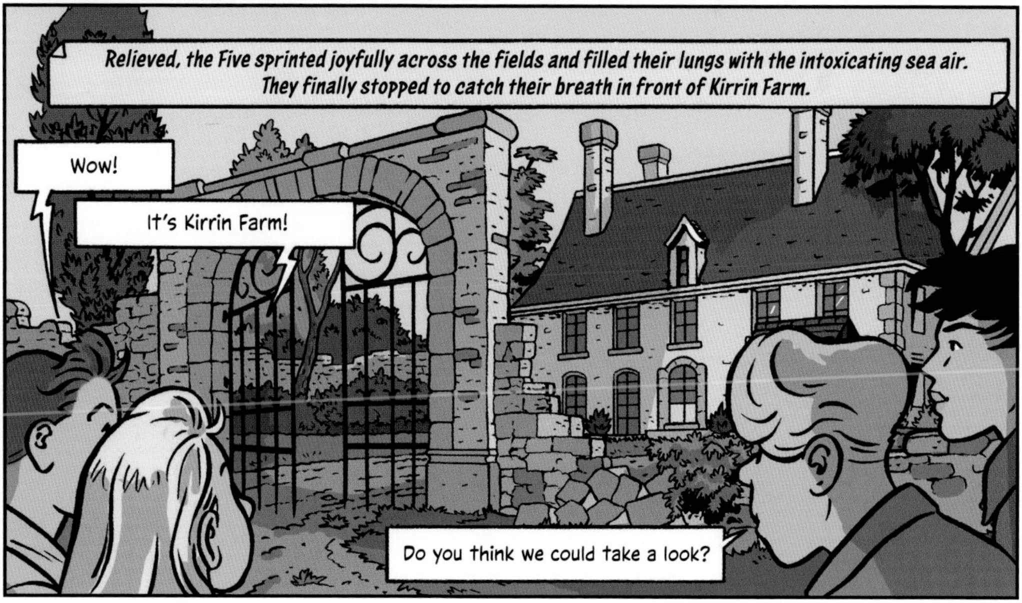
Relieved, the Five sprinted joyfully across the fields and filled their lungs with the intoxicating sea air. They finally stopped to catch their breath in front of Kirrin Farm.
Wow!
It's Kirrin Farm!
Do you think we could take a look?

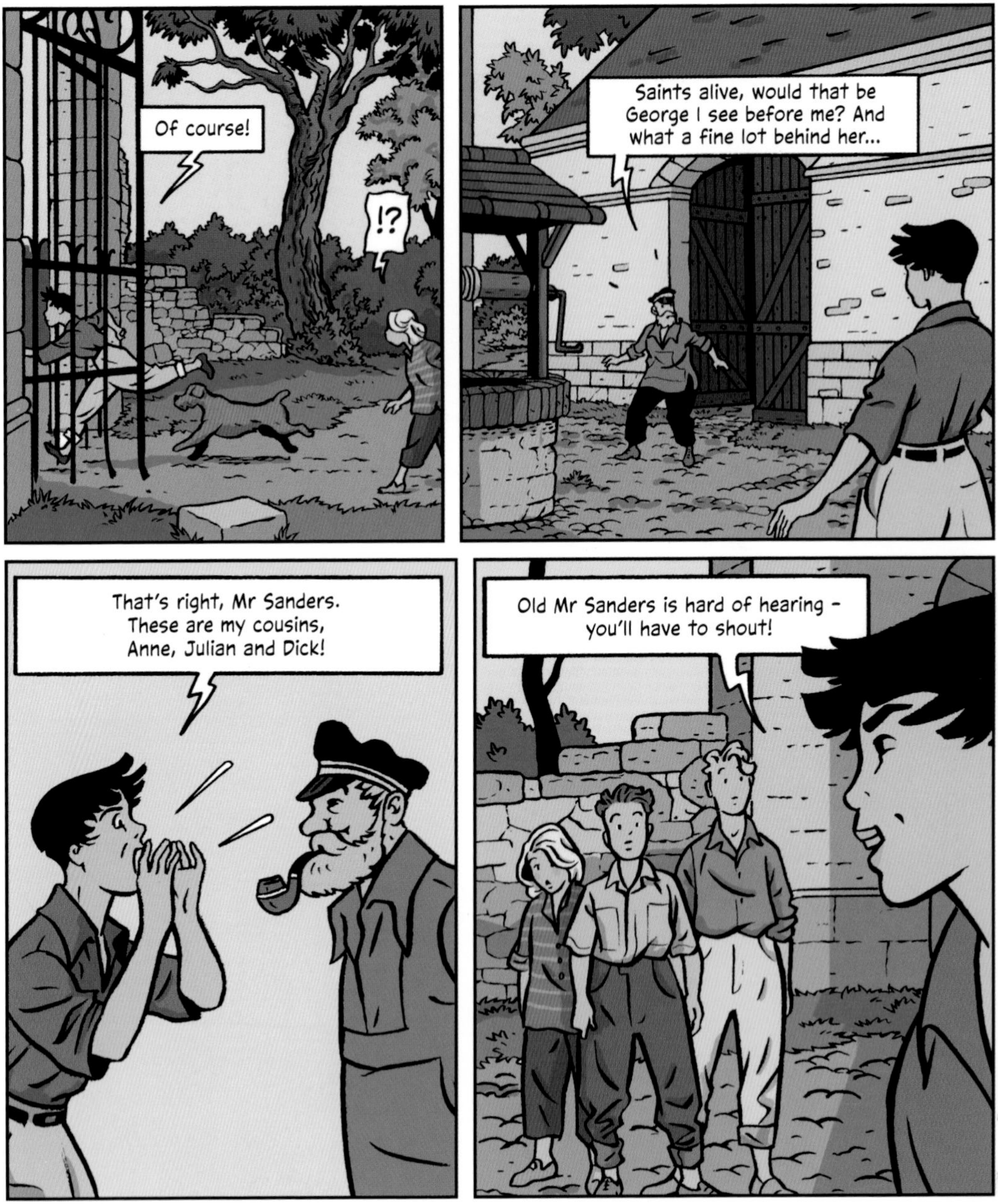
Of course!
!?
Saints alive, would that be George I see before me? And what a fine lot behind her...
That's right, Mr Sanders. These are my cousins, Anne, Julian and Dick!
Old Mr Sanders is hard of hearing – you'll have to shout!

Hello, handsome... Good ol' Timmy, sweet as pie, hee hee... Now go on in and say hello to the missus. Saints alive, she'll be over the moon when she sees ye!

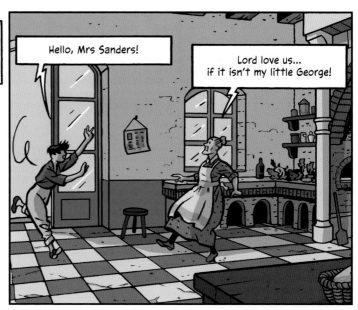

Hello, Mrs Sanders!

Lord love us... if it isn't my little George!

Ye never change, do ye? Sets my heart a-flutter to see ye here... Good job I'm strong as an ox or a shock like this'd do me in!

I do love it when my favourite rascal comes by... but, as I live and breathe, have you brought friends?

These are my cousins, Julian...

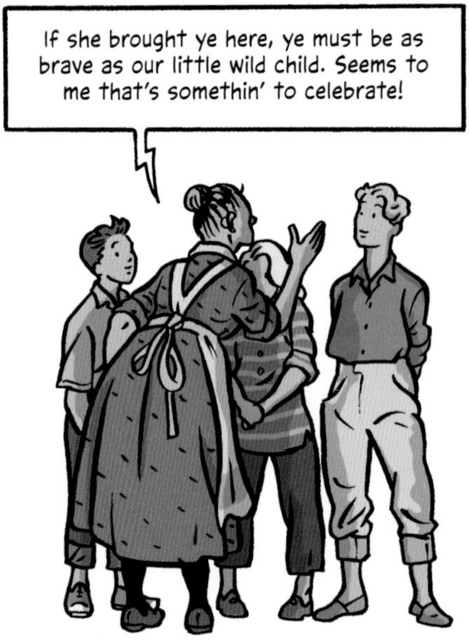
If she brought ye here, ye must be as brave as our little wild child. Seems to me that's somethin' to celebrate!

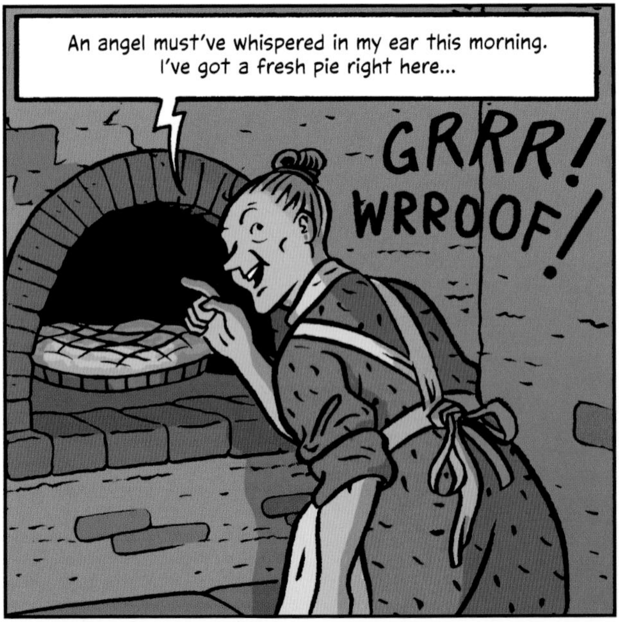
An angel must've whispered in my ear this morning. I've got a fresh pie right here...
GRRRR!
WRROOF!

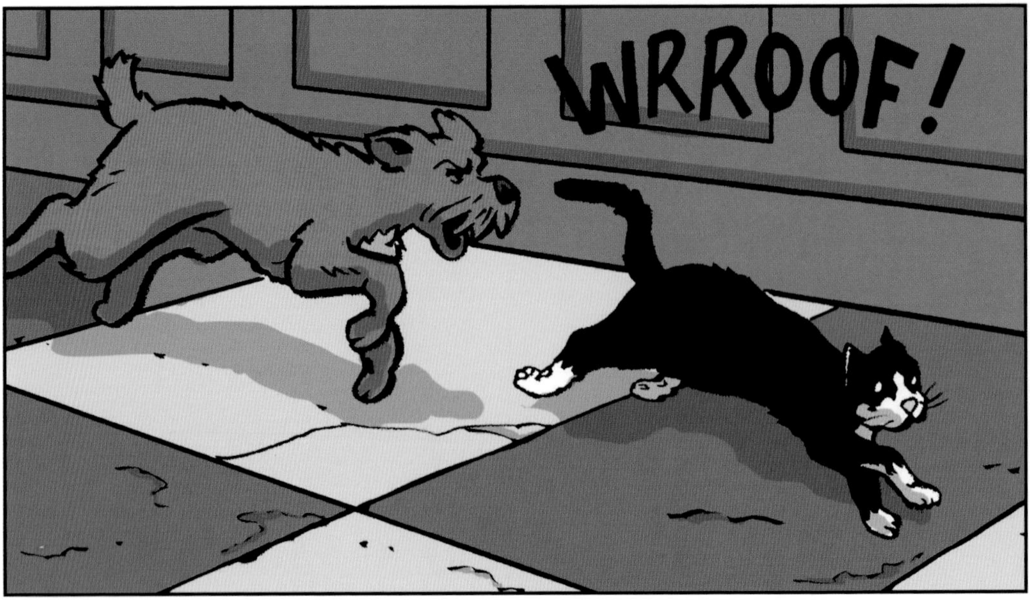
WRROOF!

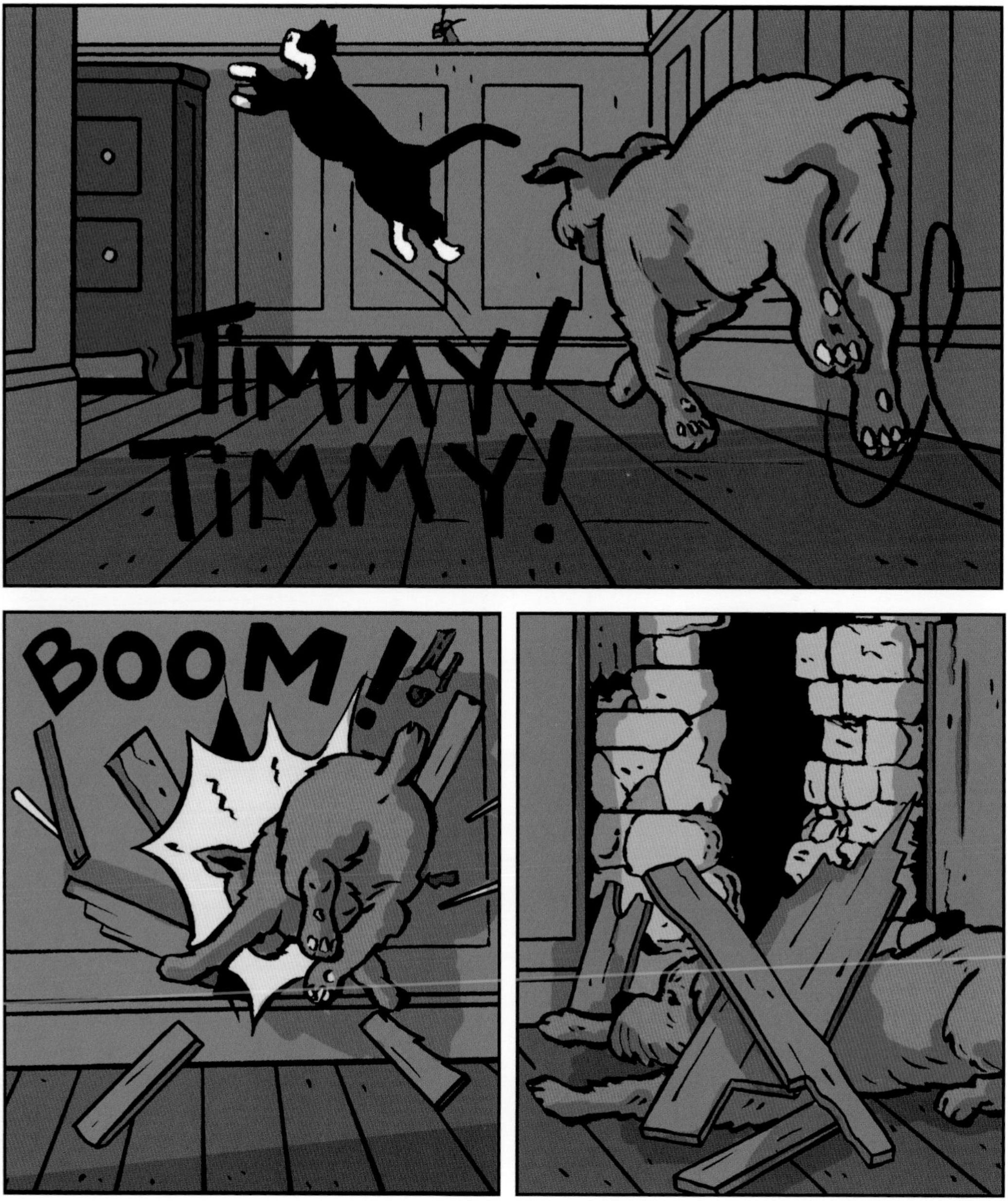
TIMMY! TIMMY!
BOOM!

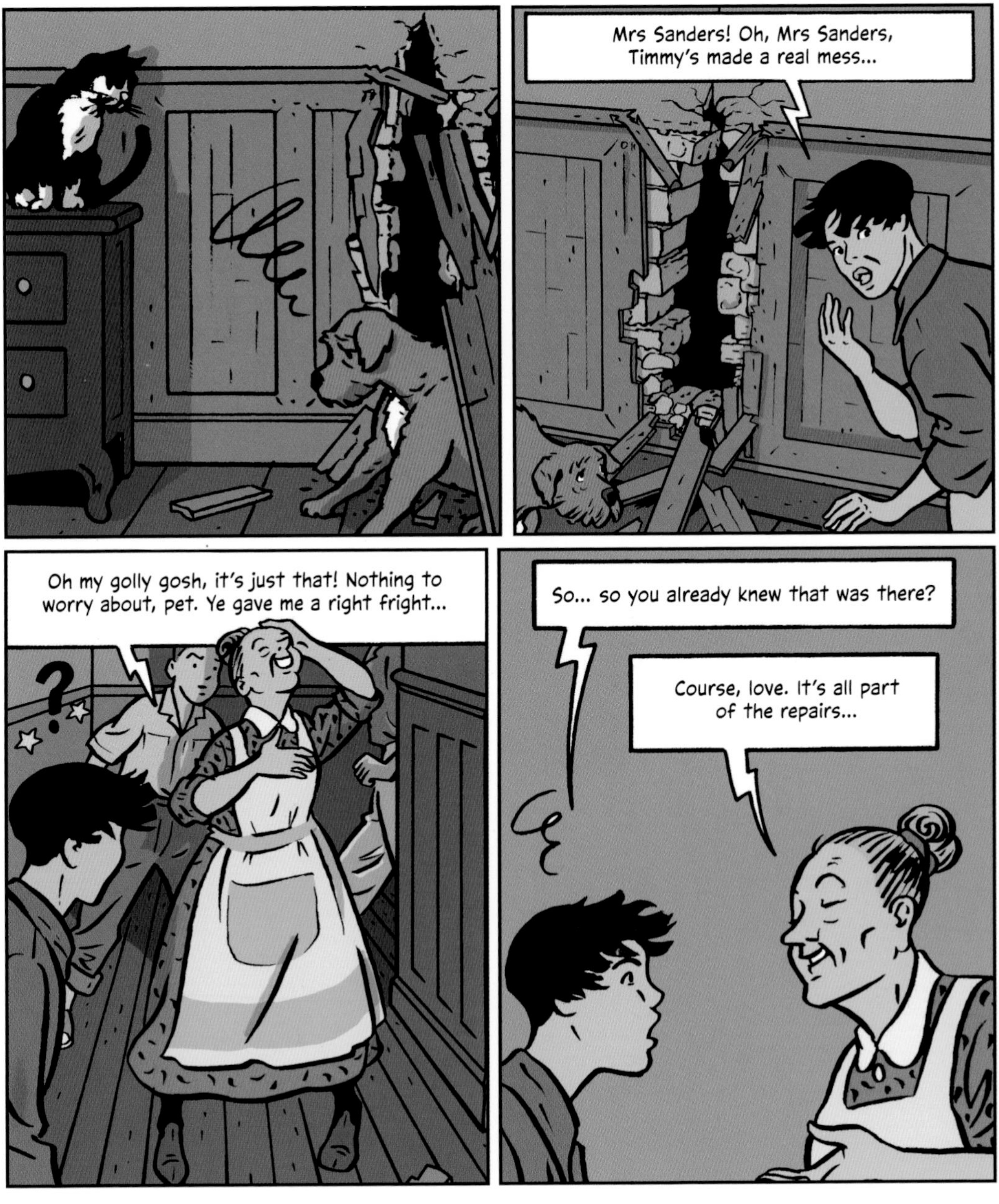
Mrs Sanders! Oh, Mrs Sanders, Timmy's made a real mess...
Oh my golly gosh, it's just that! Nothing to worry about, pet. Ye gave me a right fright...
So... so you already knew that was there?
Course, love. It's all part of the repairs...

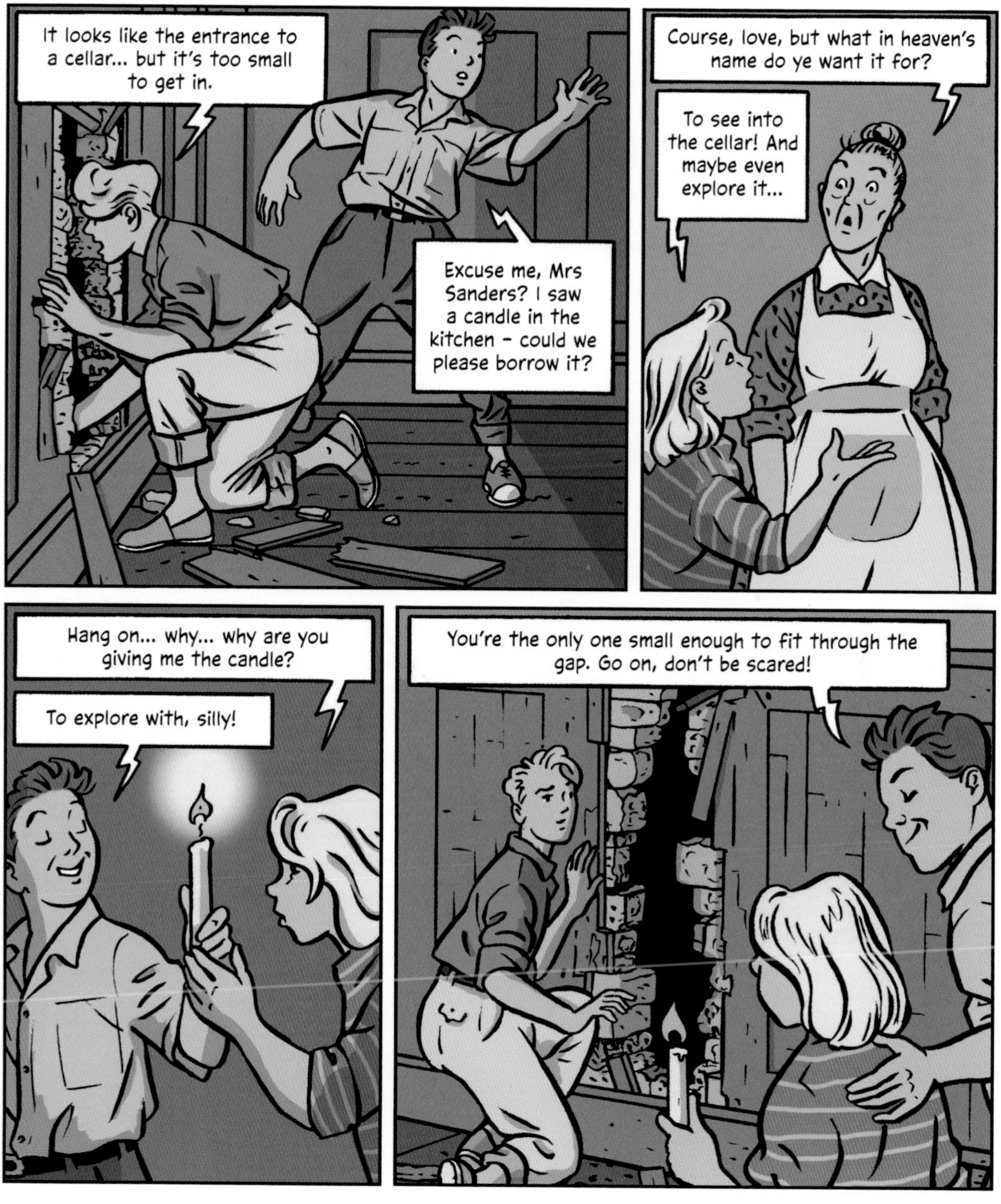
It looks like the entrance to a cellar... but it's too small to get in.
Excuse me, Mrs Sanders? I saw a candle in the kitchen – could we please borrow it?
Course, love, but what in heaven's name do ye want it for?
To see into the cellar! And maybe even explore it...
Hang on... why... why are you giving me the candle?
To explore with, silly!
You're the only one small enough to fit through the gap. Go on, don't be scared!

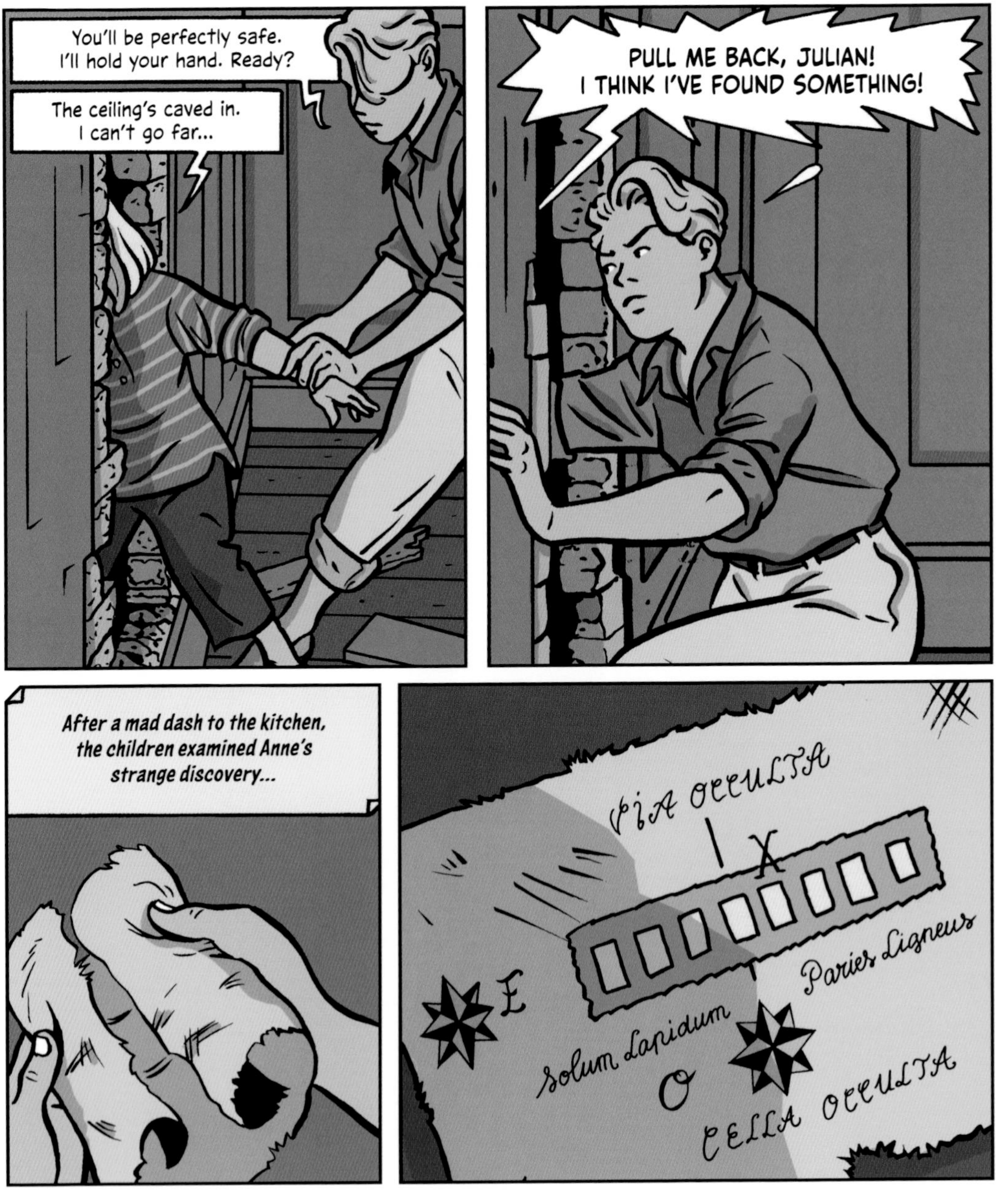
You'll be perfectly safe. I'll hold your hand. Ready?
The ceiling's caved in. I can't go far...
PULL ME BACK, JULIAN! I THINK I'VE FOUND SOMETHING!
After a mad dash to the kitchen, the children examined Anne's strange discovery...
VIA OCCULTA
I X
E
O
Solum Lapidum
Paries Ligneus
CELLA OCCULTA

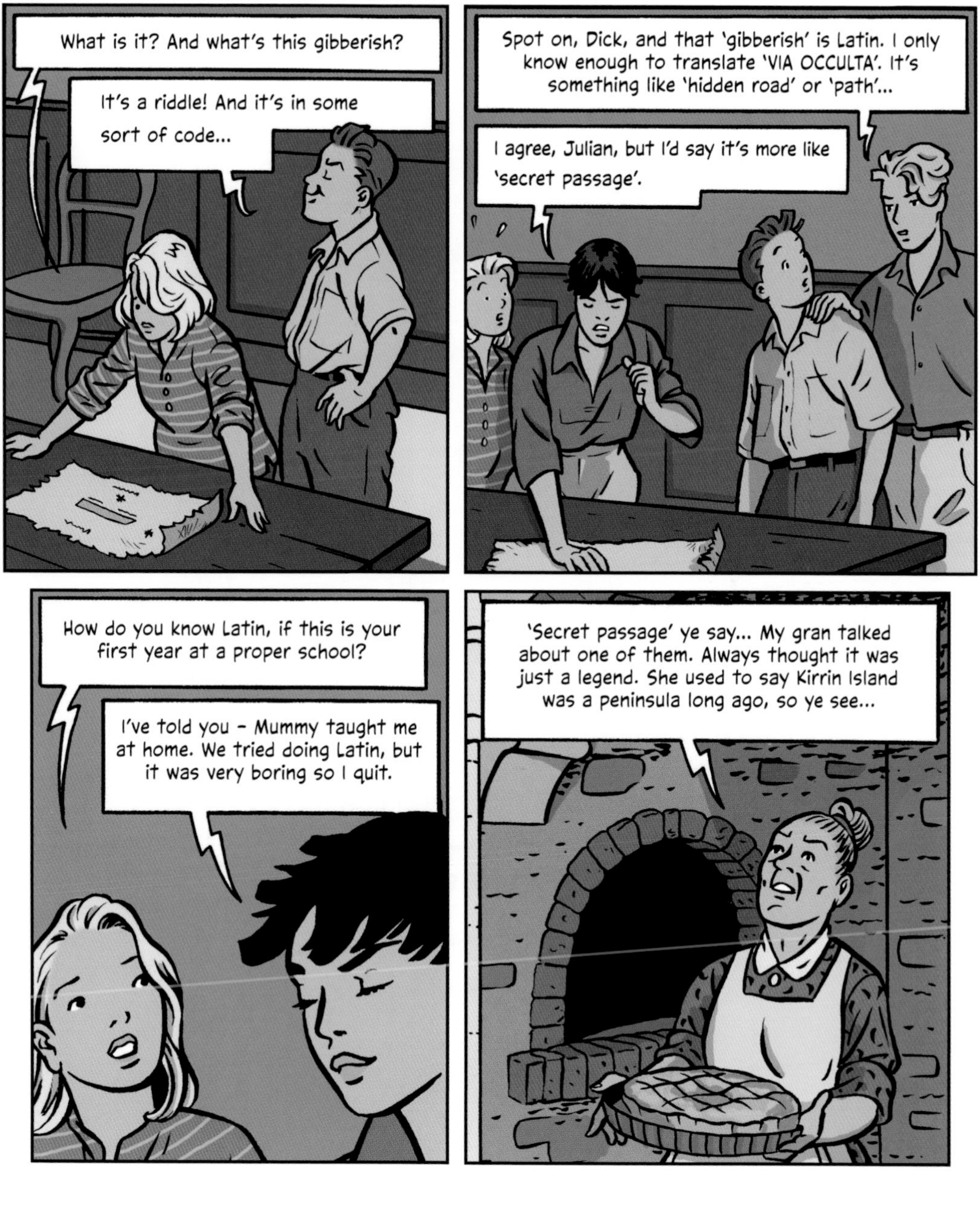
What is it? And what's this gibberish?
It's a riddle! And it's in some sort of code...
Spot on, Dick, and that 'gibberish' is Latin. I only know enough to translate 'VIA OCCULTA'. It's something like 'hidden road' or 'path'...
I agree, Julian, but I'd say it's more like 'secret passage'.
How do you know Latin, if this is your first year at a proper school?
I've told you – Mummy taught me at home. We tried doing Latin, but it was very boring so I quit.
'Secret passage' ye say... My gran talked about one of them. Always thought it was just a legend. She used to say Kirrin Island was a peninsula long ago, so ye see...

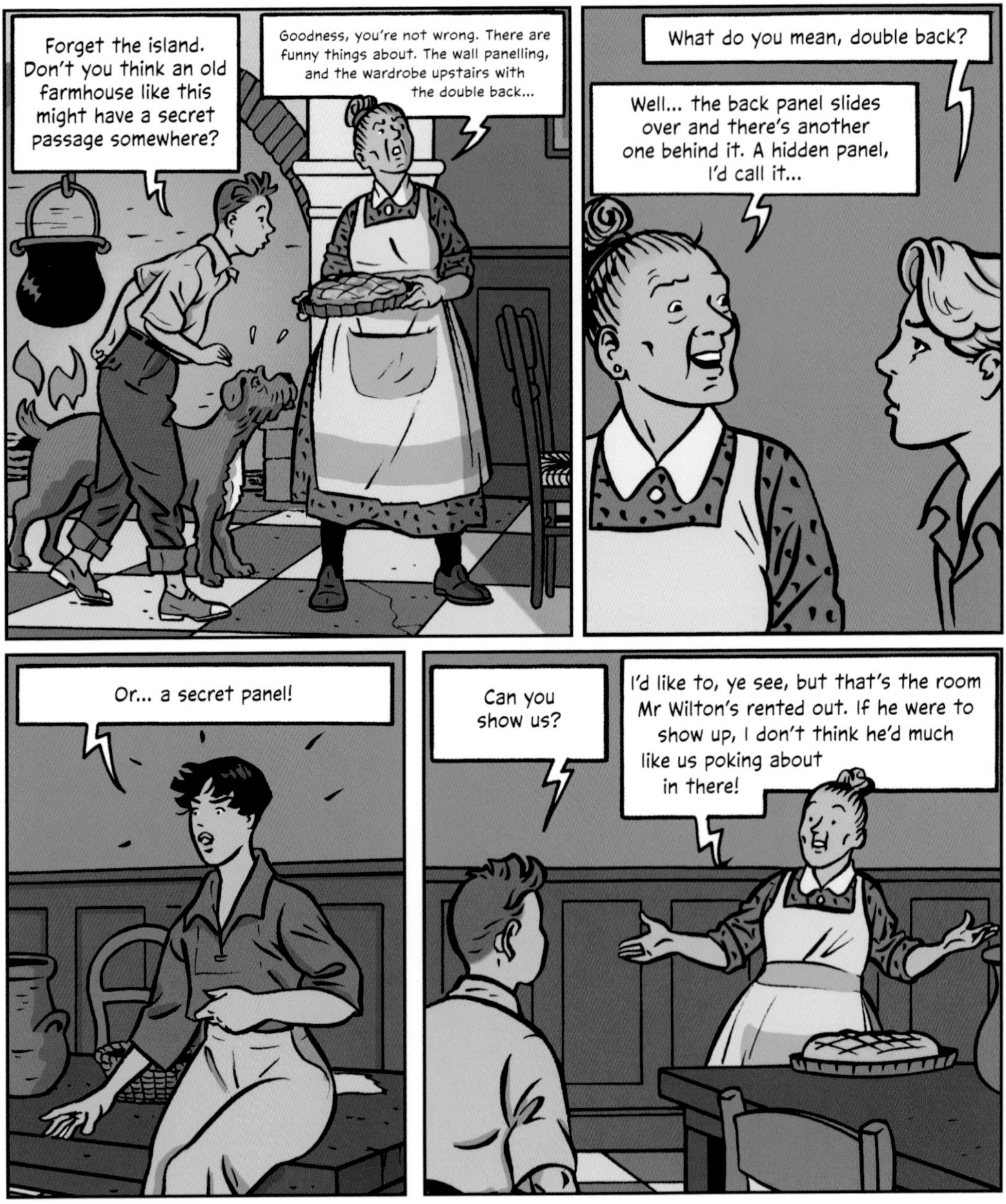
Forget the island. Don't you think an old farmhouse like this might have a secret passage somewhere?
Goodness, you're not wrong. There are funny things about. The wall panelling, and the wardrobe upstairs with the double back...
What do you mean, double back?
Well... the back panel slides over and there's another one behind it. A hidden panel, I'd call it...
Or... a secret panel!
Can you show us?
I'd like to, ye see, but that's the room Mr Wilton's rented out. If he were to show up, I don't think he'd much like us poking about in there!

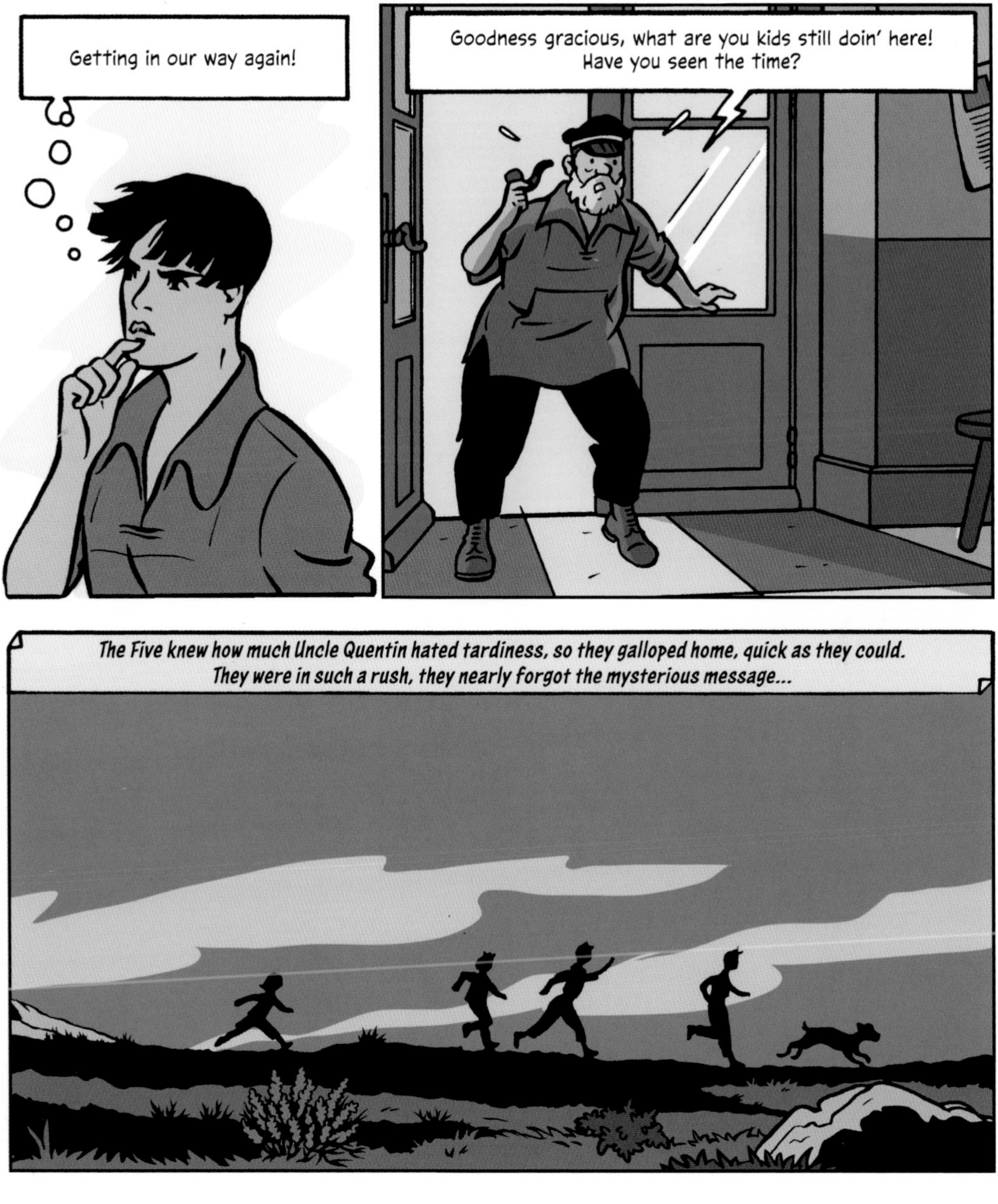
Getting in our way again!
Goodness gracious, what are you kids still doin' here! Have you seen the time?
The Five knew how much Uncle Quentin hated tardiness, so they galloped home, quick as they could. They were in such a rush, they nearly forgot the mysterious message...

Ah, you're finally here! You're lucky Quentin's in a good mood. He's had a lovely chat with Mr Roland. Your tutor is also a bit of a radar fanatic, it turns out...

Our what?

Our tutor, George. He's here to make sure we revise over the holidays.

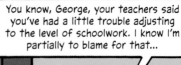

You know, George, your teachers said you've had a little trouble adjusting to the level of schoolwork. I know I'm partially to blame for that...

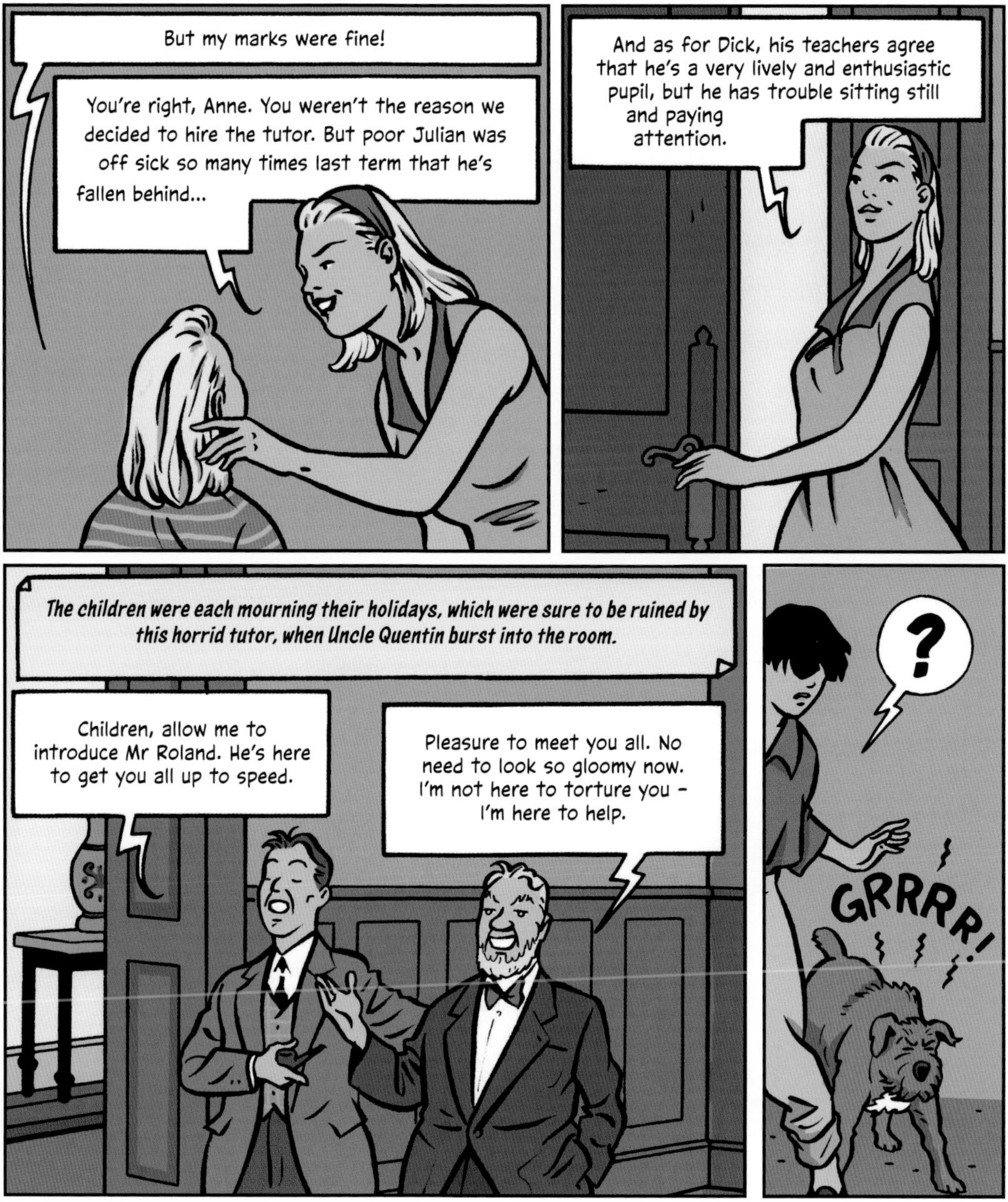

But my marks were fine!
You're right, Anne. You weren't the reason we decided to hire the tutor. But poor Julian was off sick so many times last term that he's fallen behind...
And as for Dick, his teachers agree that he's a very lively and enthusiastic pupil, but he has trouble sitting still and paying attention.
The children were each mourning their holidays, which were sure to be ruined by this horrid tutor, when Uncle Quentin burst into the room.
Children, allow me to introduce Mr Roland. He's here to get you all up to speed.
Pleasure to meet you all. No need to look so gloomy now. I'm not here to torture you – I'm here to help.
?
GRRRR!

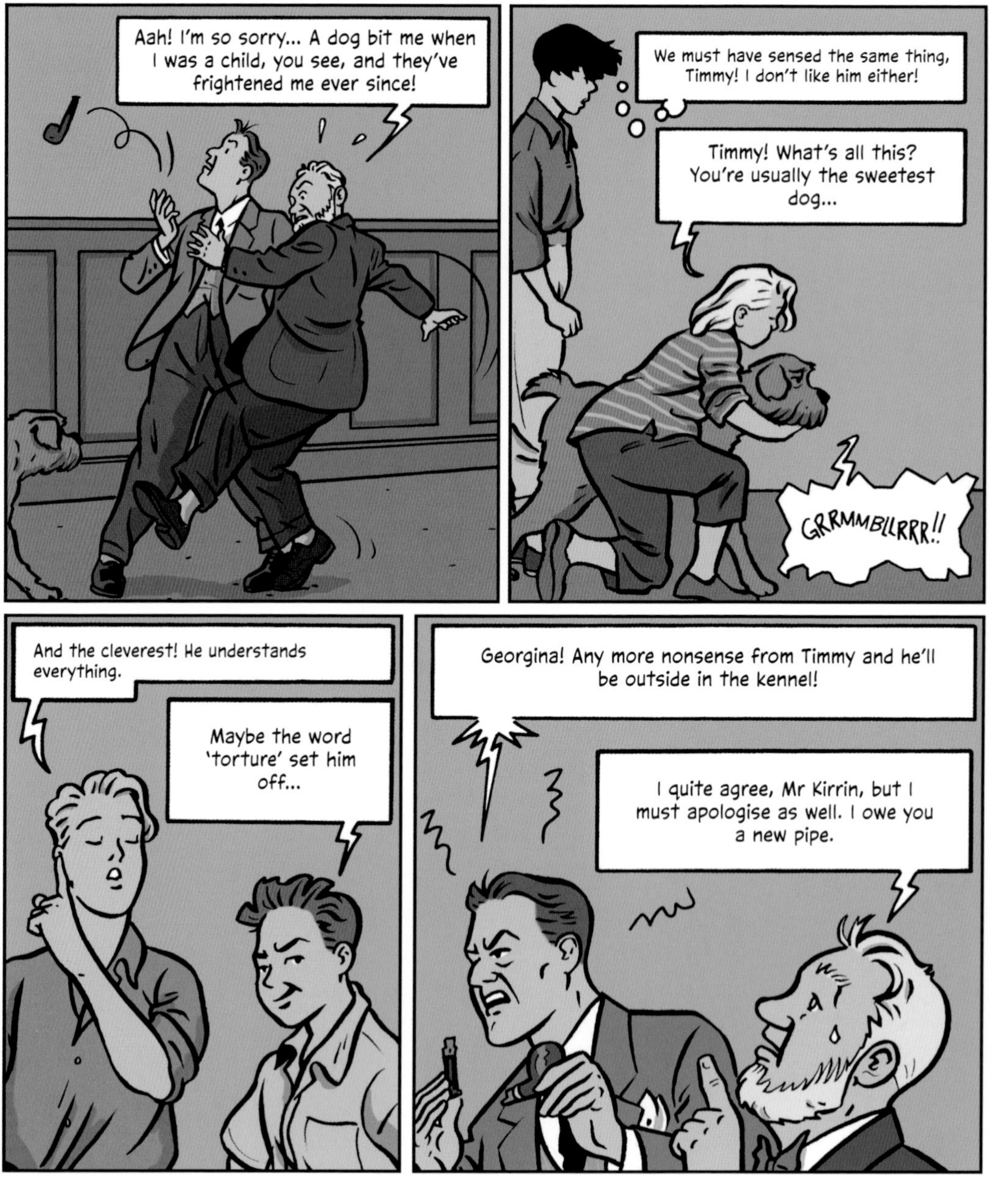
Aah! I'm so sorry... A dog bit me when I was a child, you see, and they've frightened me ever since!
We must have sensed the same thing, Timmy! I don't like him either!
Timmy! What's all this? You're usually the sweetest dog...
GRRMMBLLRRR!!
And the cleverest! He understands everything.
Maybe the word 'torture' set him off...
Georgina! Any more nonsense from Timmy and he'll be outside in the kennel!
I quite agree, Mr Kirrin, but I must apologise as well. I owe you a new pipe.

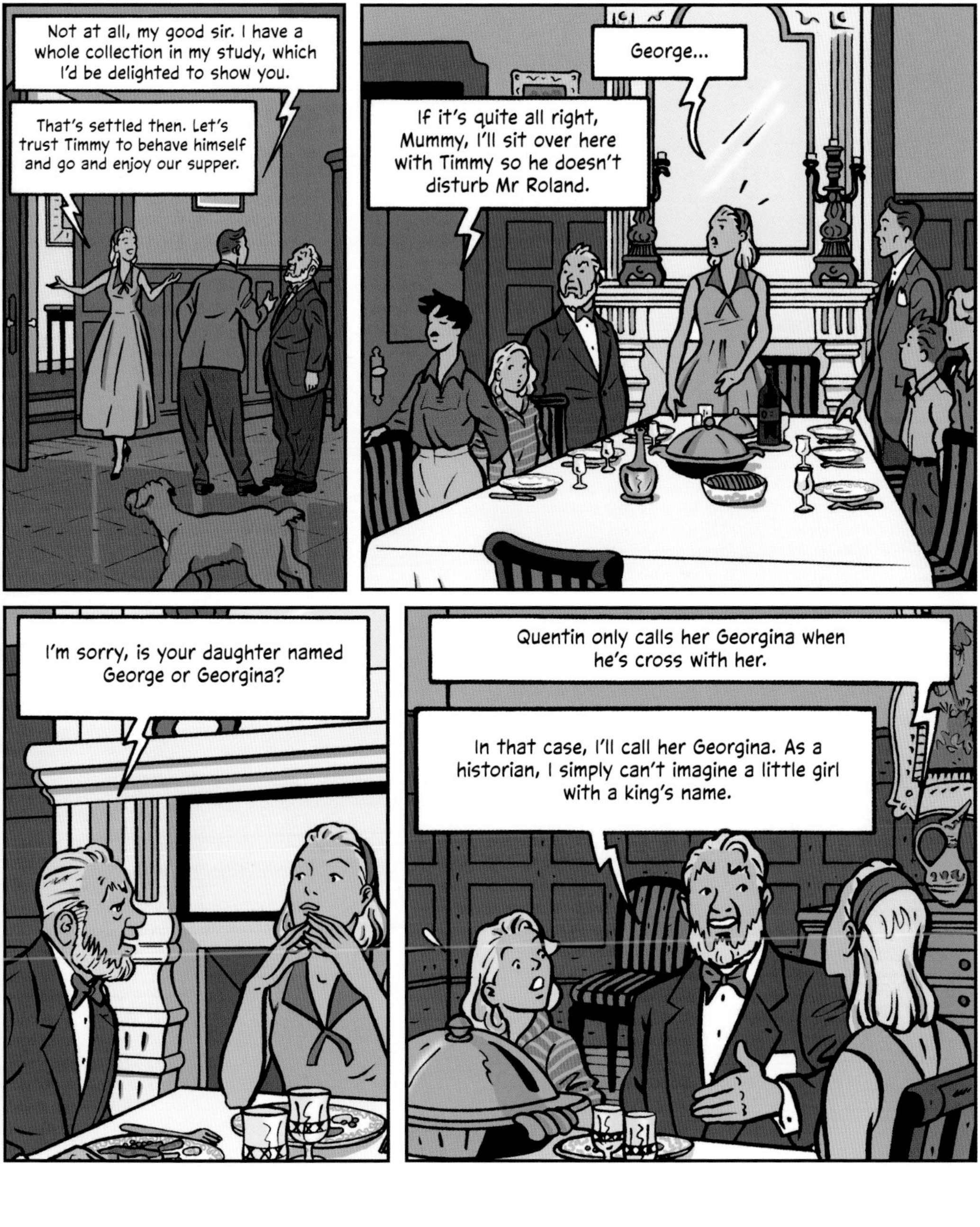
Not at all, my good sir. I have a whole collection in my study, which I'd be delighted to show you.
That's settled then. Let's trust Timmy to behave himself and go and enjoy our supper.
George...
If it's quite all right, Mummy, I'll sit over here with Timmy so he doesn't disturb Mr Roland.
I'm sorry, is your daughter named George or Georgina?
Quentin only calls her Georgina when he's cross with her.
In that case, I'll call her Georgina. As a historian, I simply can't imagine a little girl with a king's name.

You're a teacher, you can help us with the Latin...

OWW!!

??!!

THUD!

That wretched dog again!

It's not Timmy, sir, it was me... I mean, my leg...

Well done, Dick. Anne nearly let the cat out of the bag.

Sometimes it just goes stiff all on its own. Mummy says it's growing pains...

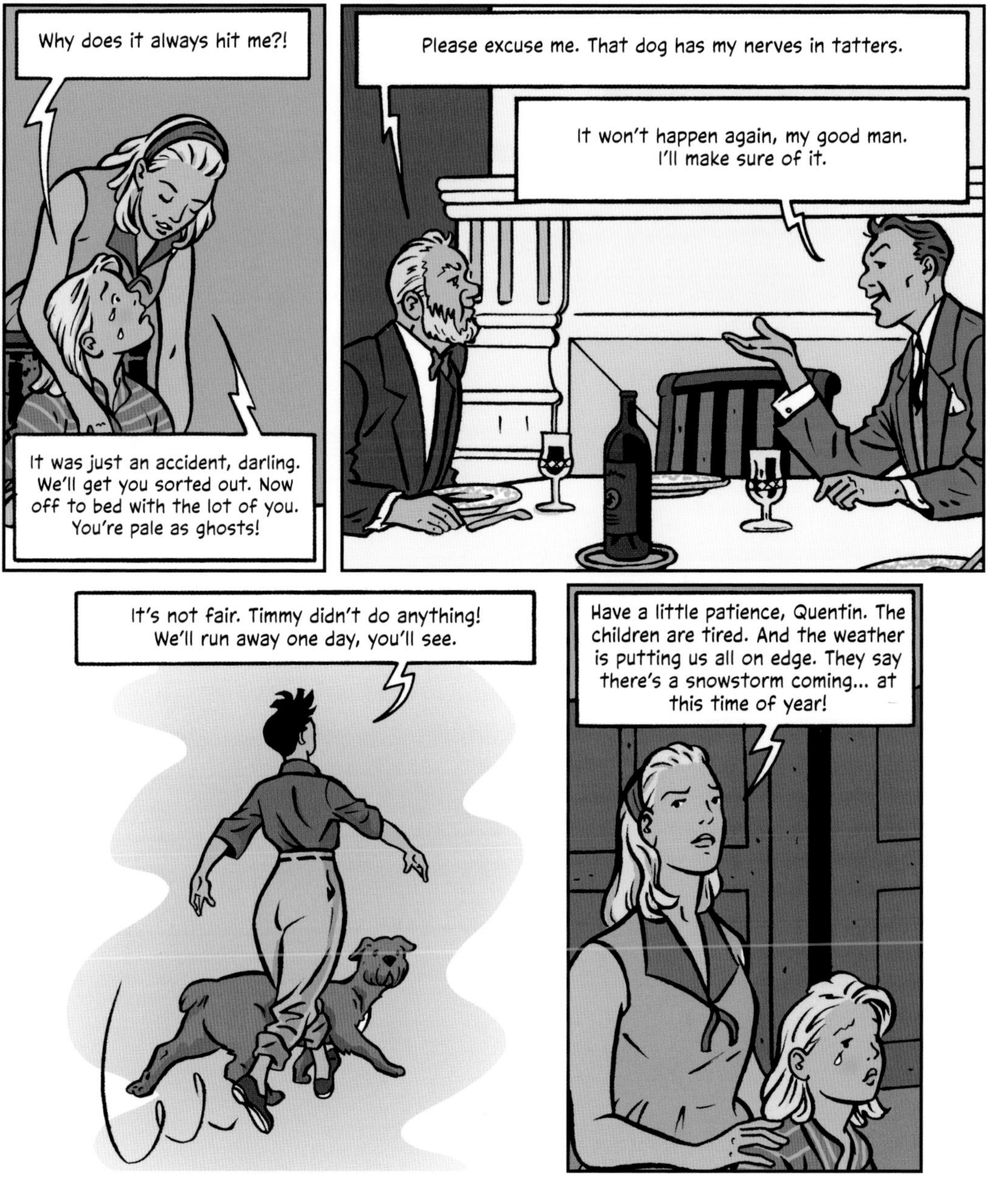
Why does it always hit me?!
It was just an accident, darling. We'll get you sorted out. Now off to bed with the lot of you. You're pale as ghosts!
Please excuse me. That dog has my nerves in tatters.
It won't happen again, my good man. I'll make sure of it.
It's not fair. Timmy didn't do anything! We'll run away one day, you'll see.
Have a little patience, Quentin. The children are tired. And the weather is putting us all on edge. They say there's a snowstorm coming... at this time of year!

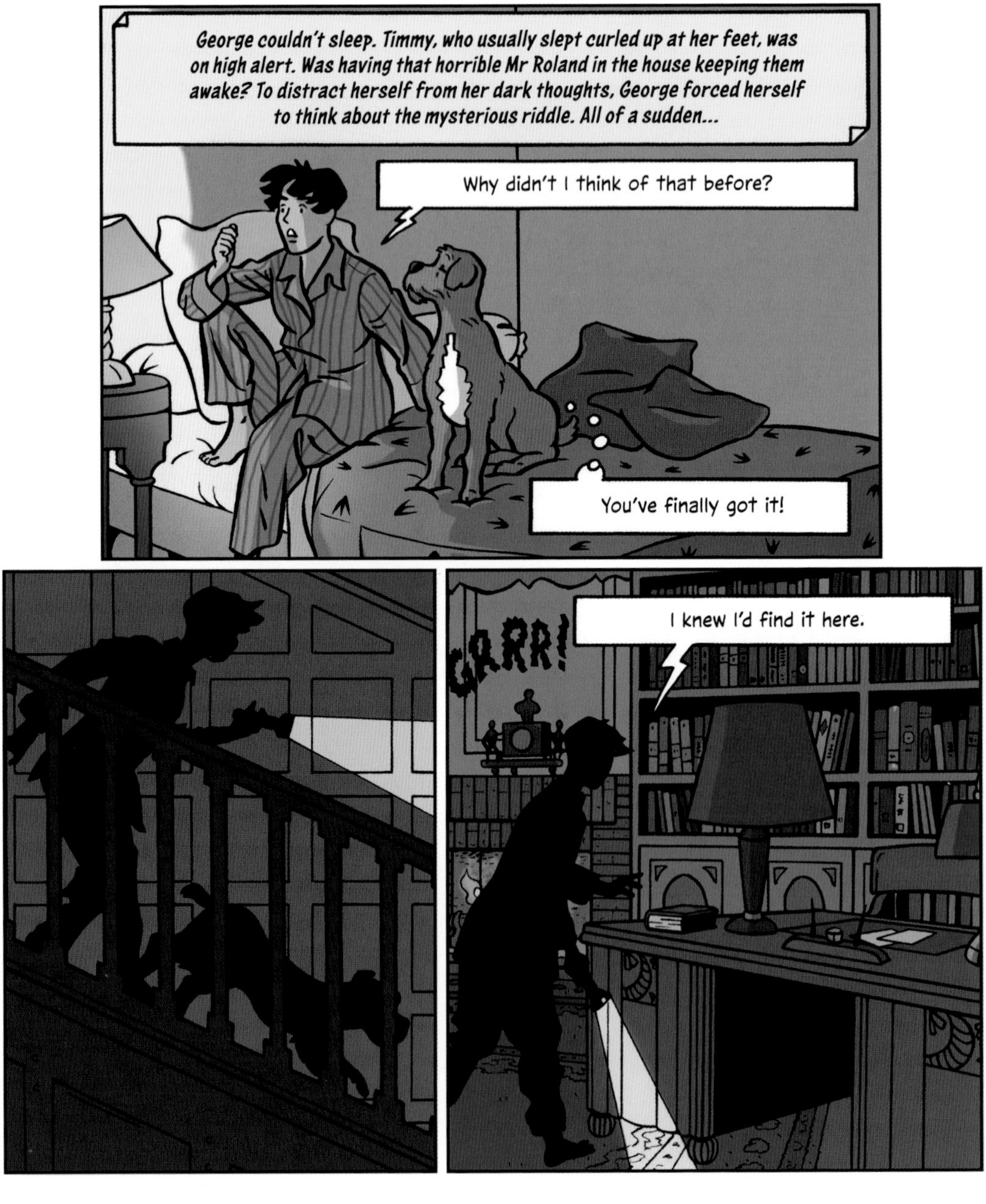
George couldn't sleep. Timmy, who usually slept curled up at her feet, was on high alert. Was having that horrible Mr Roland in the house keeping them awake? To distract herself from her dark thoughts, George forced herself to think about the mysterious riddle. All of a sudden...
Why didn't I think of that before?
You've finally got it!
GRRR!
I knew I'd find it here.

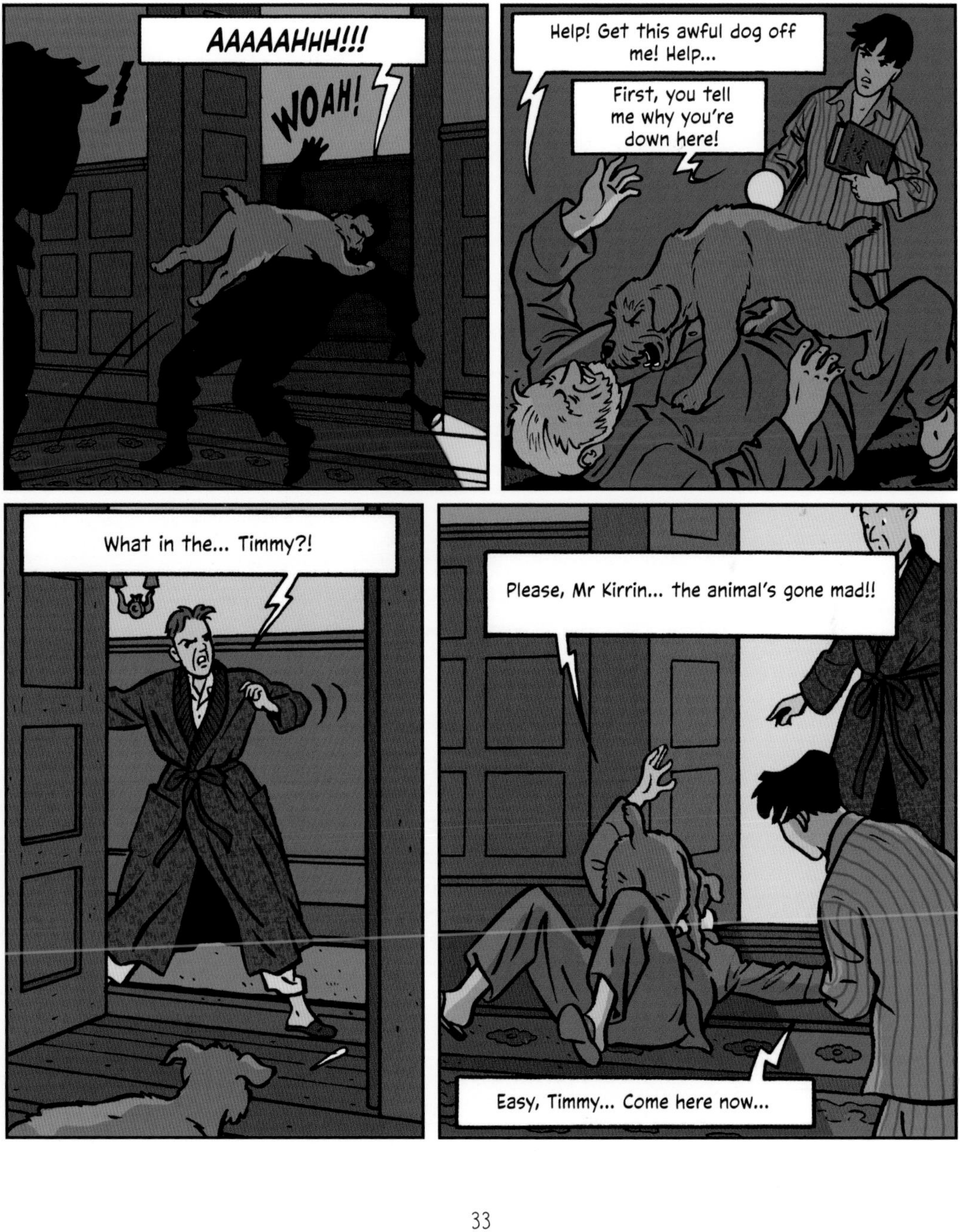
AAAAAHHH!!!
!
WOAH!
Help! Get this awful dog off me! Help...
First, you tell me why you're down here!
What in the... Timmy?!
Please, Mr Kirrin... the animal's gone mad!!
Easy, Timmy... Come here now...

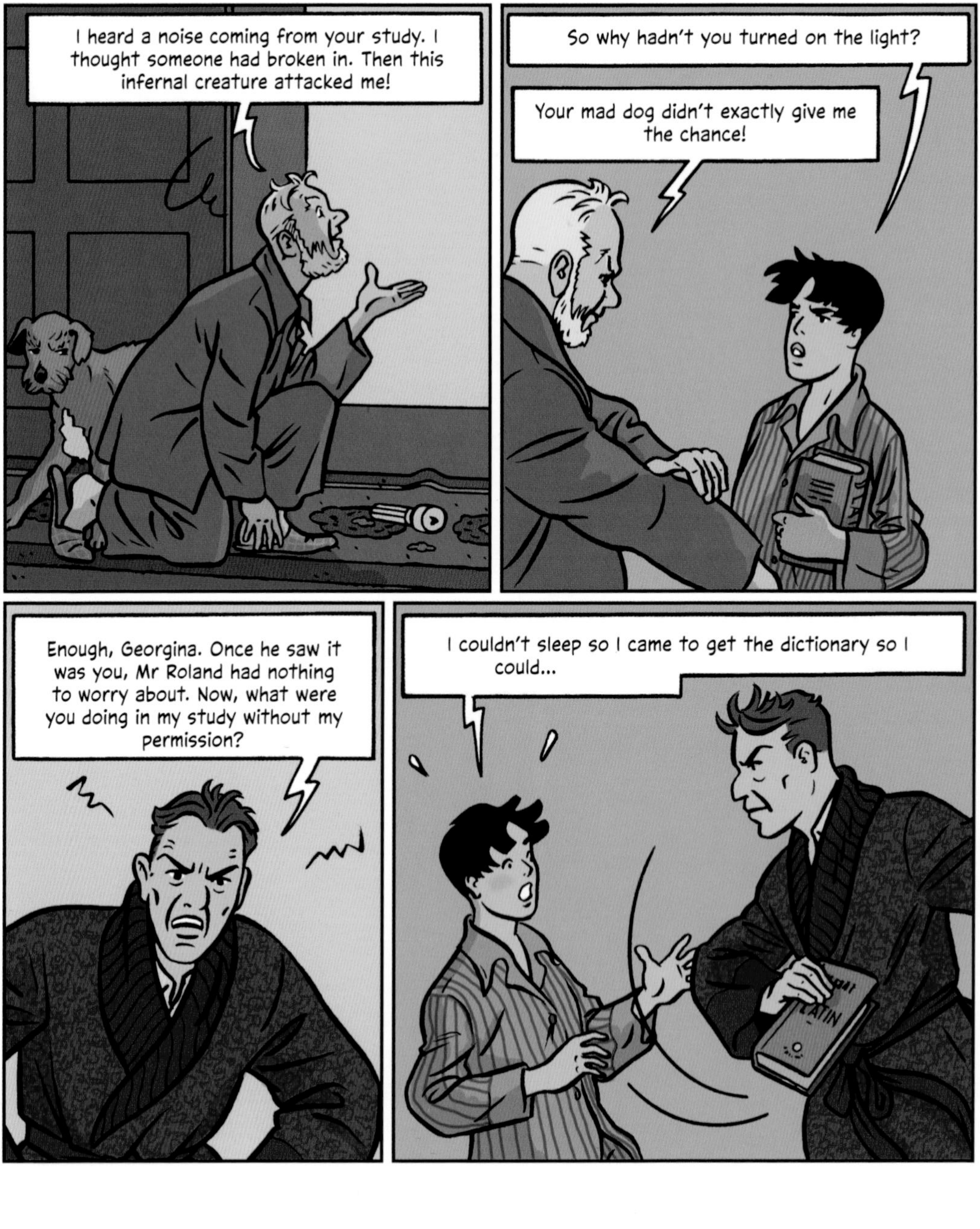
I heard a noise coming from your study. I thought someone had broken in. Then this infernal creature attacked me!
So why hadn't you turned on the light?
Your mad dog didn't exactly give me the chance!
Enough, Georgina. Once he saw it was you, Mr Roland had nothing to worry about. Now, what were you doing in my study without my permission?
I couldn't sleep so I came to get the dictionary so I could...
LATIN

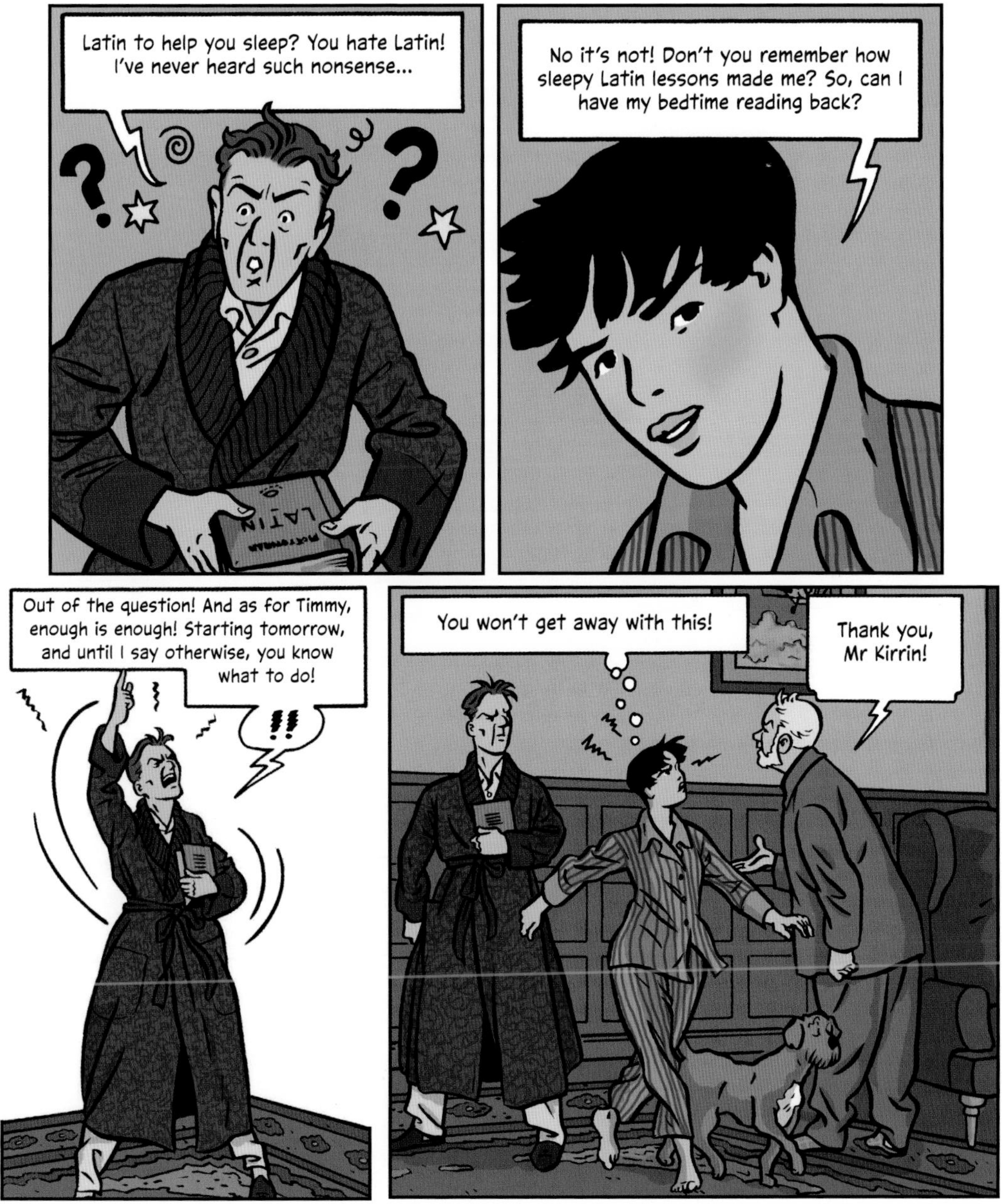
Latin to help you sleep? You hate Latin! I've never heard such nonsense...
LATIN
No it's not! Don't you remember how sleepy Latin lessons made me? So, can I have my bedtime reading back?
Out of the question! And as for Timmy, enough is enough! Starting tomorrow, and until I say otherwise, you know what to do!
!!
You won't get away with this!
Thank you, Mr Kirrin!

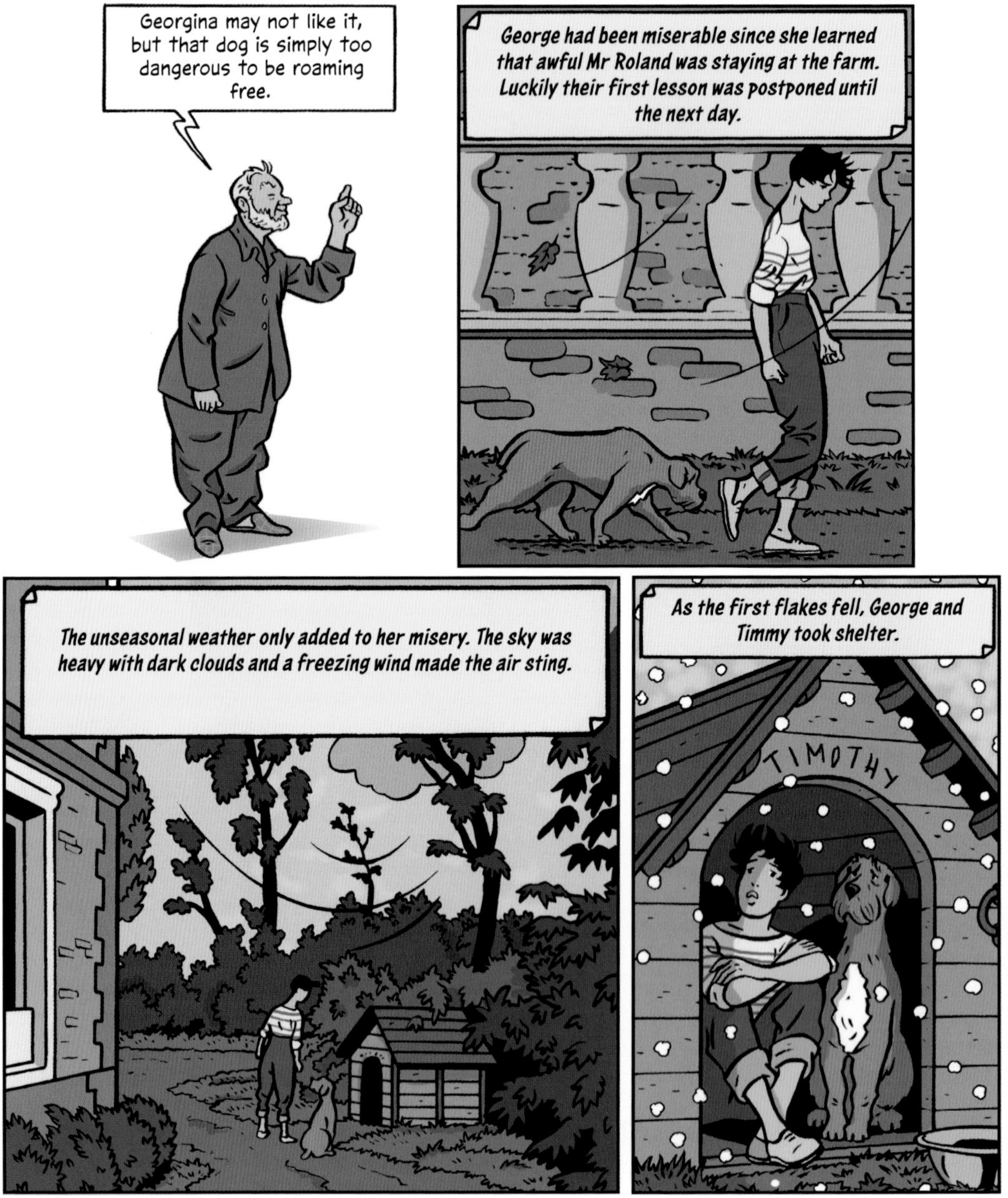
Georgina may not like it, but that dog is simply too dangerous to be roaming free.
George had been miserable since she learned that awful Mr Roland was staying at the farm. Luckily their first lesson was postponed until the next day.
The unseasonal weather only added to her misery. The sky was heavy with dark clouds and a freezing wind made the air sting.
As the first flakes fell, George and Timmy took shelter.
TIMOTHY

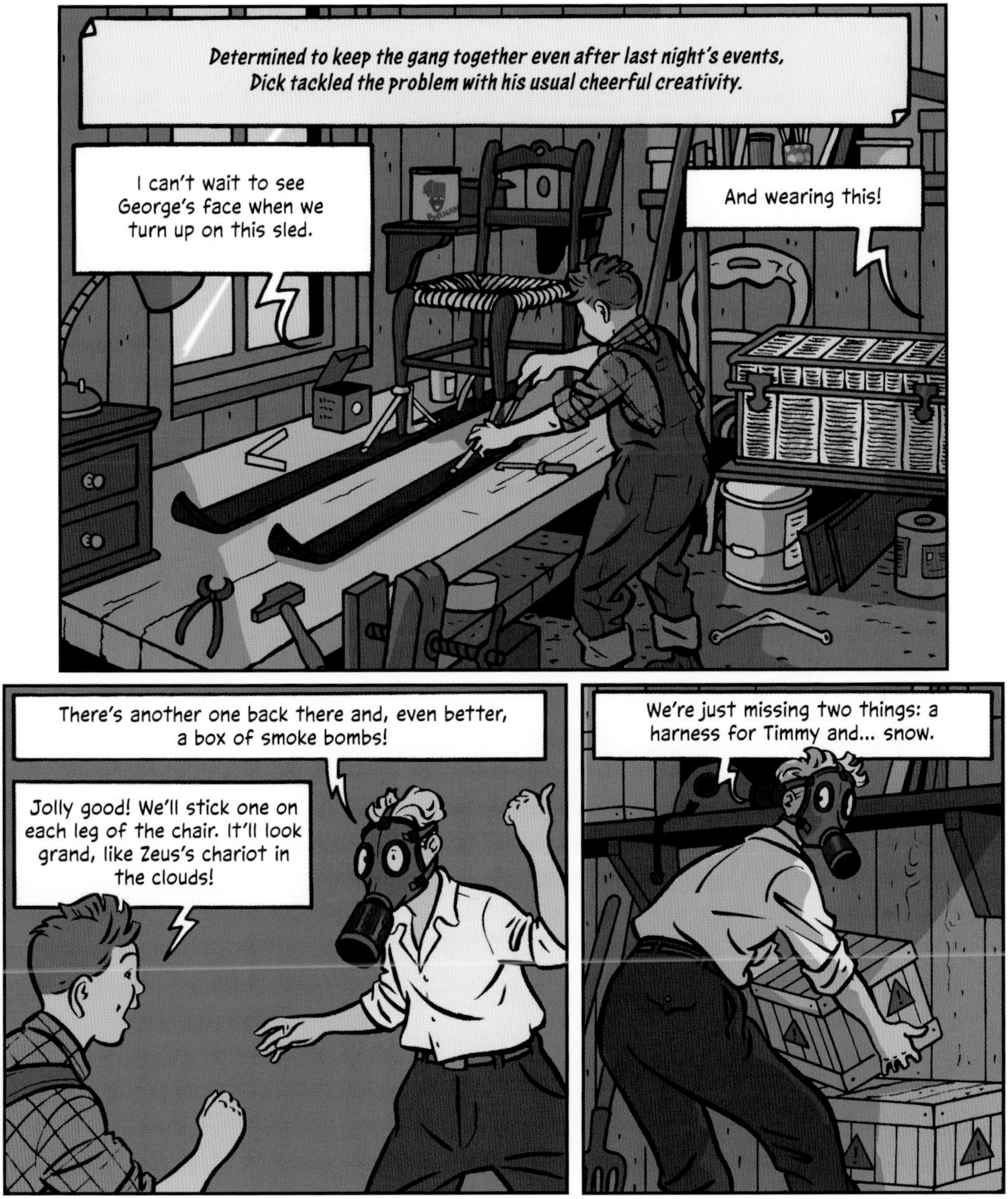
Determined to keep the gang together even after last night's events, Dick tackled the problem with his usual cheerful creativity.
I can't wait to see George's face when we turn up on this sled.
And wearing this!
There's another one back there and, even better, a box of smoke bombs!
Jolly good! We'll stick one on each leg of the chair. It'll look grand, like Zeus's chariot in the clouds!
We're just missing two things: a harness for Timmy and... snow.

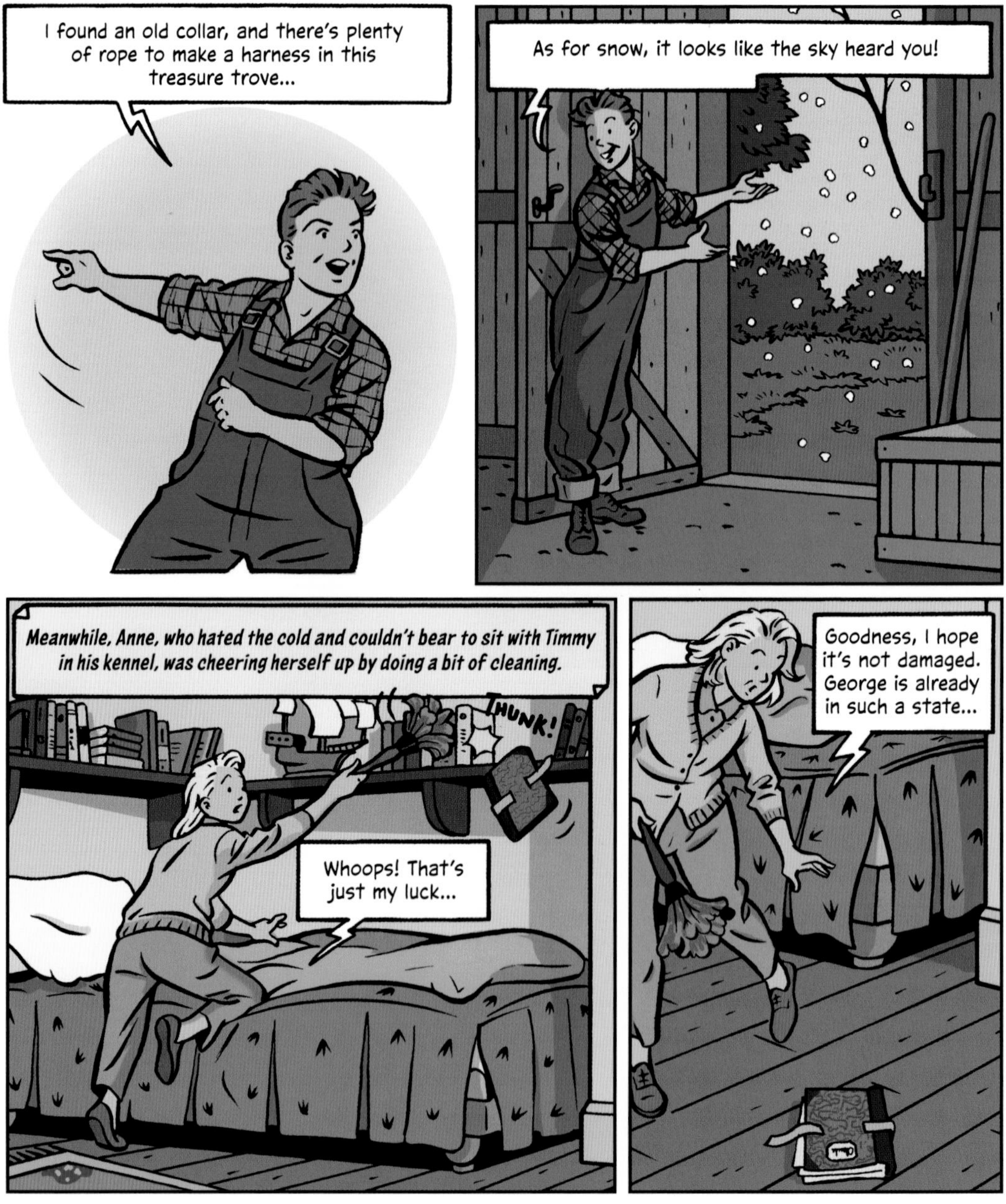
I found an old collar, and there's plenty of rope to make a harness in this treasure trove...
As for snow, it looks like the sky heard you!
Meanwhile, Anne, who hated the cold and couldn't bear to sit with Timmy in his kennel, was cheering herself up by doing a bit of cleaning.
THUNK!
Whoops! That's just my luck...
Goodness, I hope it's not damaged. George is already in such a state...

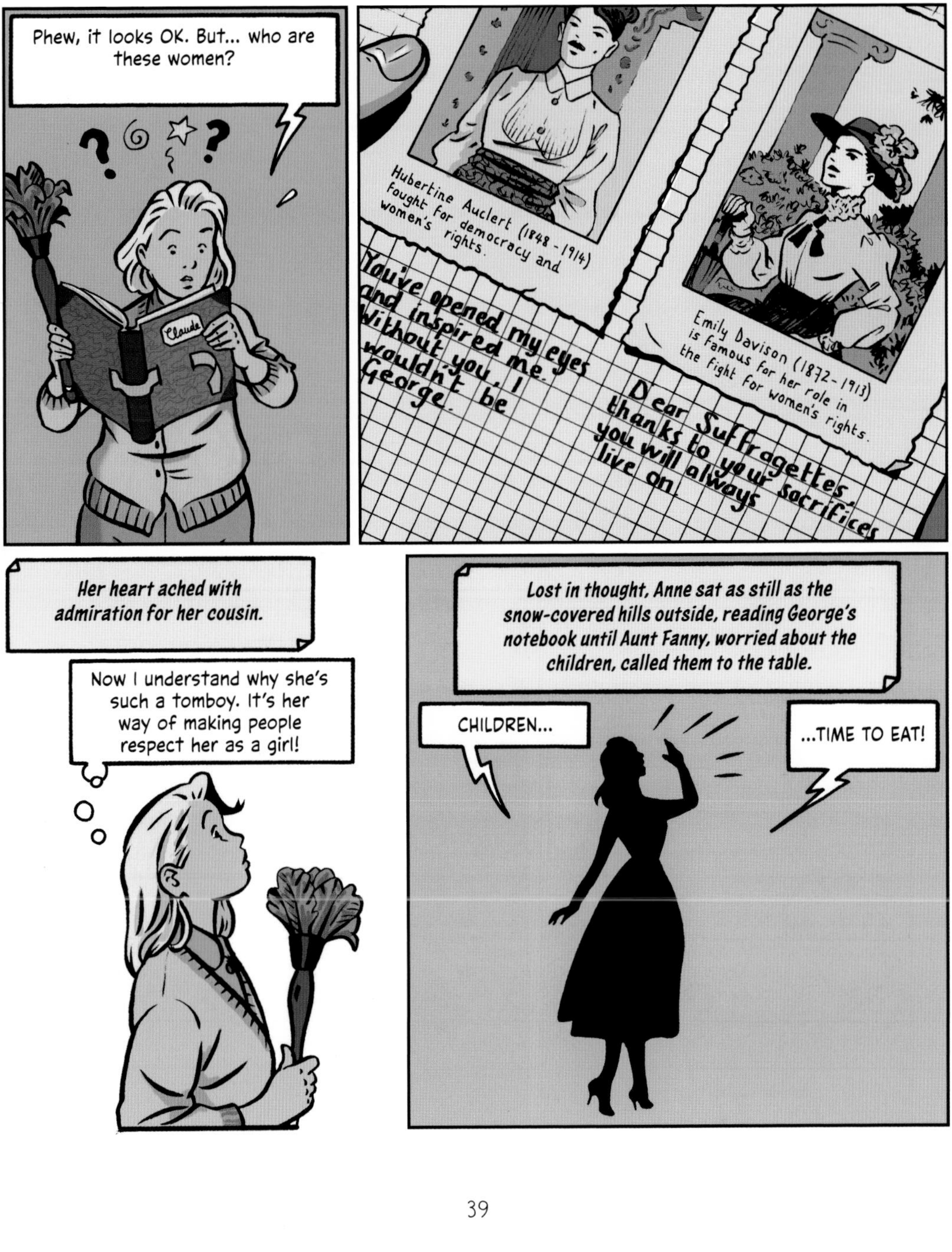

Phew, it looks OK. But... who are these women?
Claude
Hubertine Auclert (1848 - 1914) fought for democracy and women's rights.
Emily Davison (1872 - 1913) is famous for her role in the fight for women's rights.
You've opened my eyes and inspired me. Without you, I wouldn't be George.
Dear Suffragettes, thanks to your sacrifices you will always live on.
Her heart ached with admiration for her cousin.
Now I understand why she's such a tomboy. It's her way of making people respect her as a girl!
Lost in thought, Anne sat as still as the snow-covered hills outside, reading George's notebook until Aunt Fanny, worried about the children, called them to the table.
CHILDREN...
...TIME TO EAT!

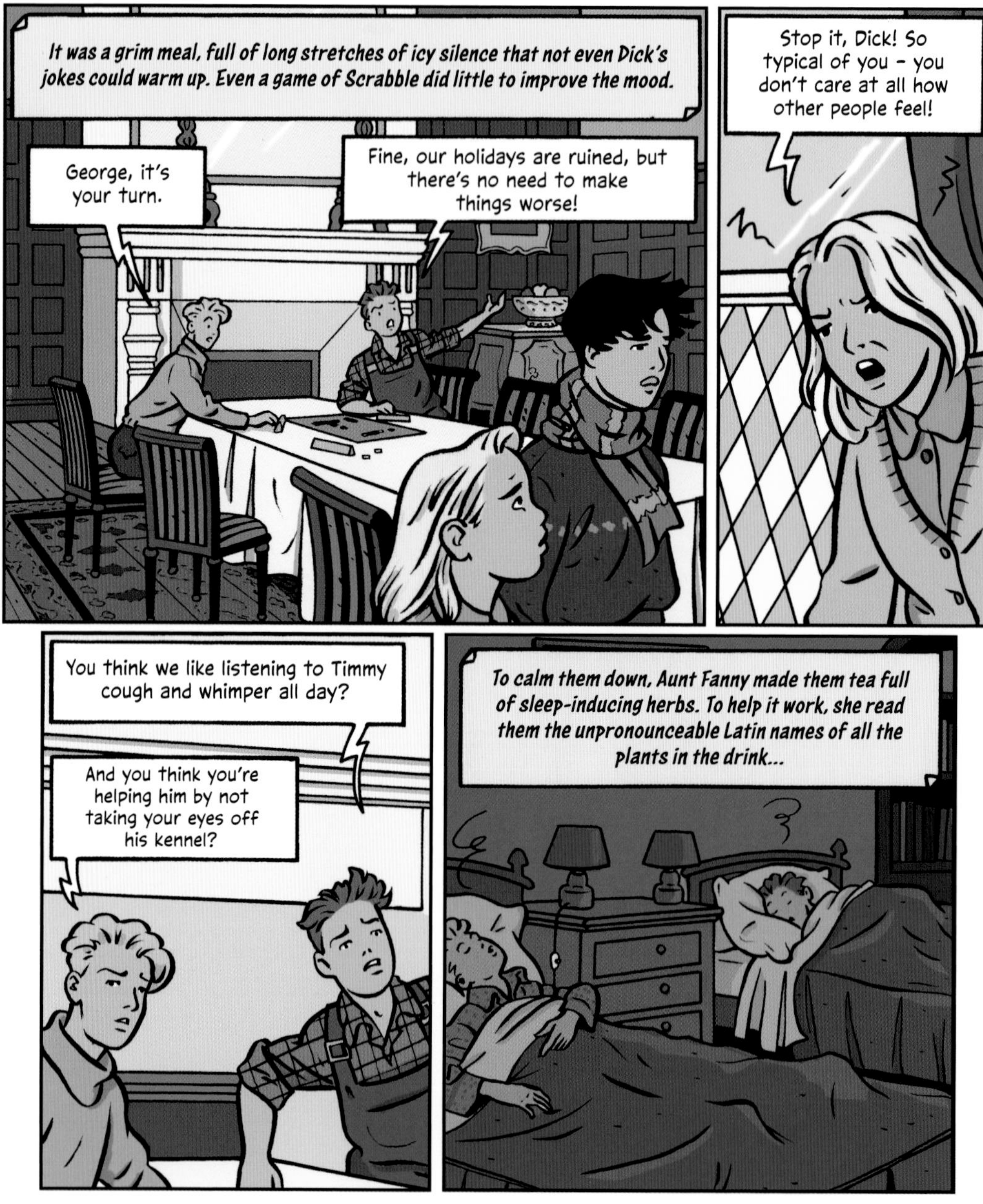
It was a grim meal, full of long stretches of icy silence that not even Dick's jokes could warm up. Even a game of Scrabble did little to improve the mood.
George, it's your turn.
Fine, our holidays are ruined, but there's no need to make things worse!
Stop it, Dick! So typical of you – you don't care at all how other people feel!
You think we like listening to Timmy cough and whimper all day?
And you think you're helping him by not taking your eyes off his kennel?
To calm them down, Aunt Fanny made them tea full of sleep-inducing herbs. To help it work, she read them the unpronounceable Latin names of all the plants in the drink...

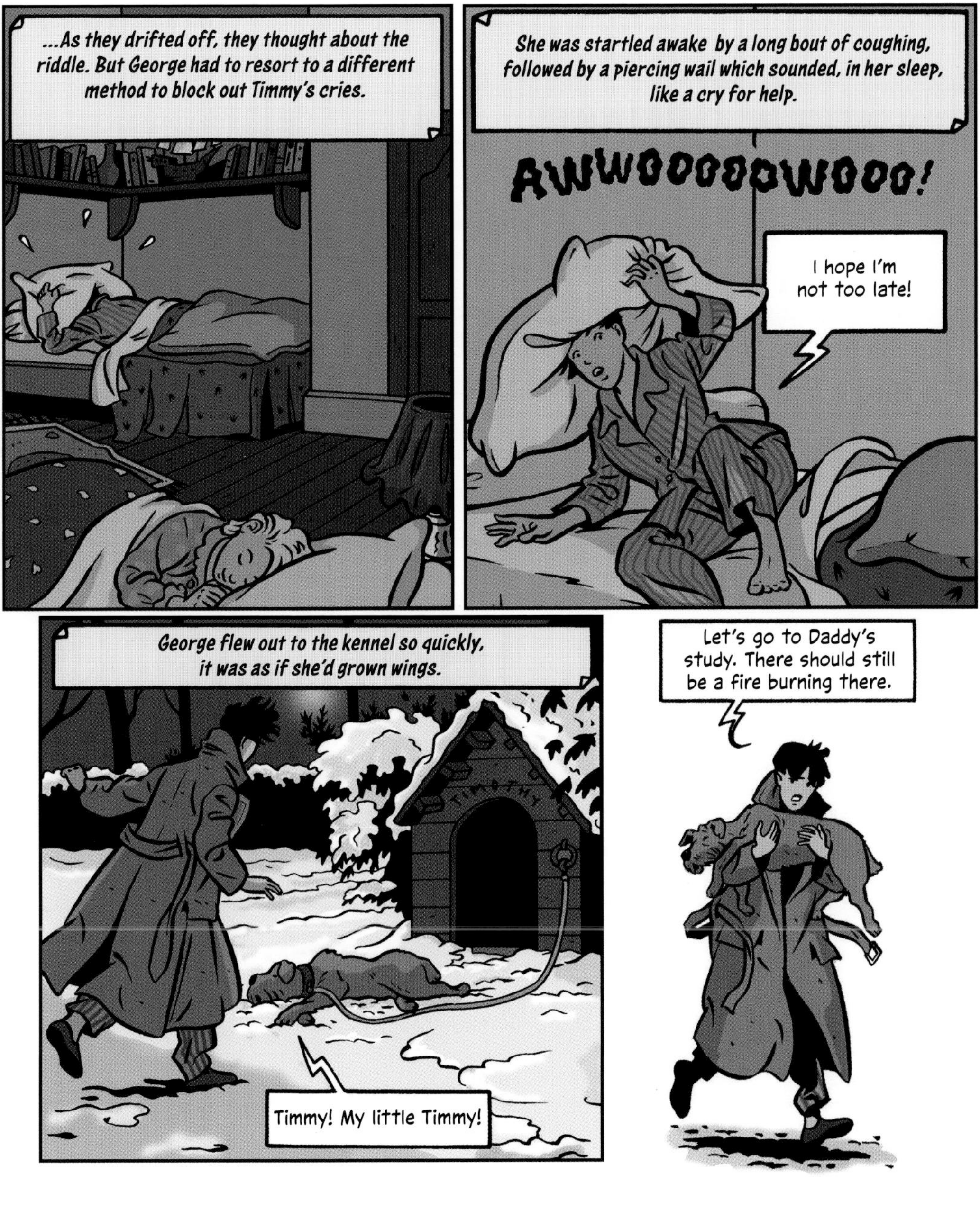
...As they drifted off, they thought about the riddle. But George had to resort to a different method to block out Timmy's cries.
She was startled awake by a long bout of coughing, followed by a piercing wail which sounded, in her sleep, like a cry for help.
AWWOOOOOWOOO!
I hope I'm not too late!
George flew out to the kennel so quickly, it was as if she'd grown wings.
TIMOTHY
Timmy! My little Timmy!
Let's go to Daddy's study. There should still be a fire burning there.

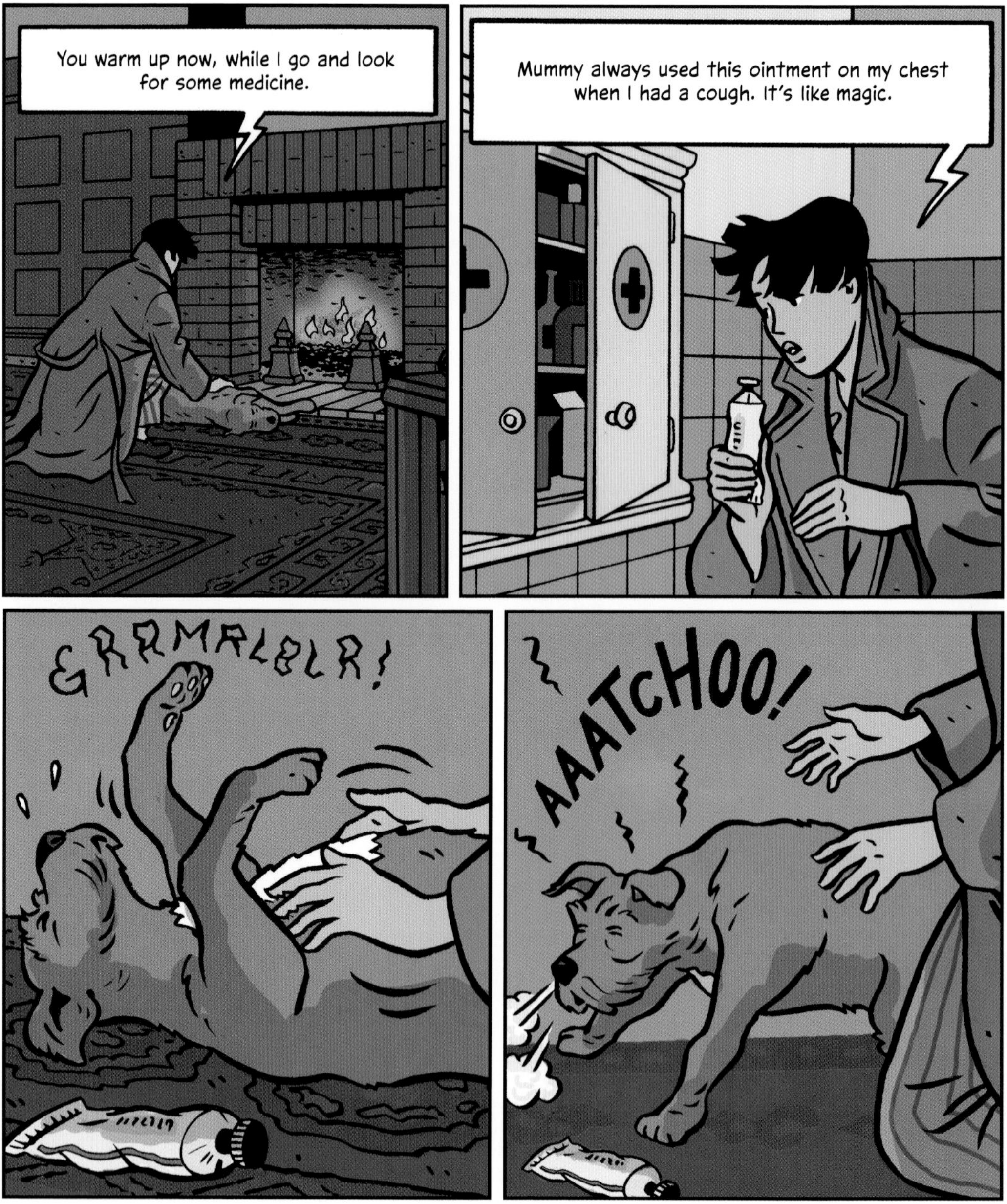
You warm up now, while I go and look for some medicine.
Mummy always used this ointment on my chest when I had a cough. It's like magic.
GRRMRLBLR!
AAATCHOO!

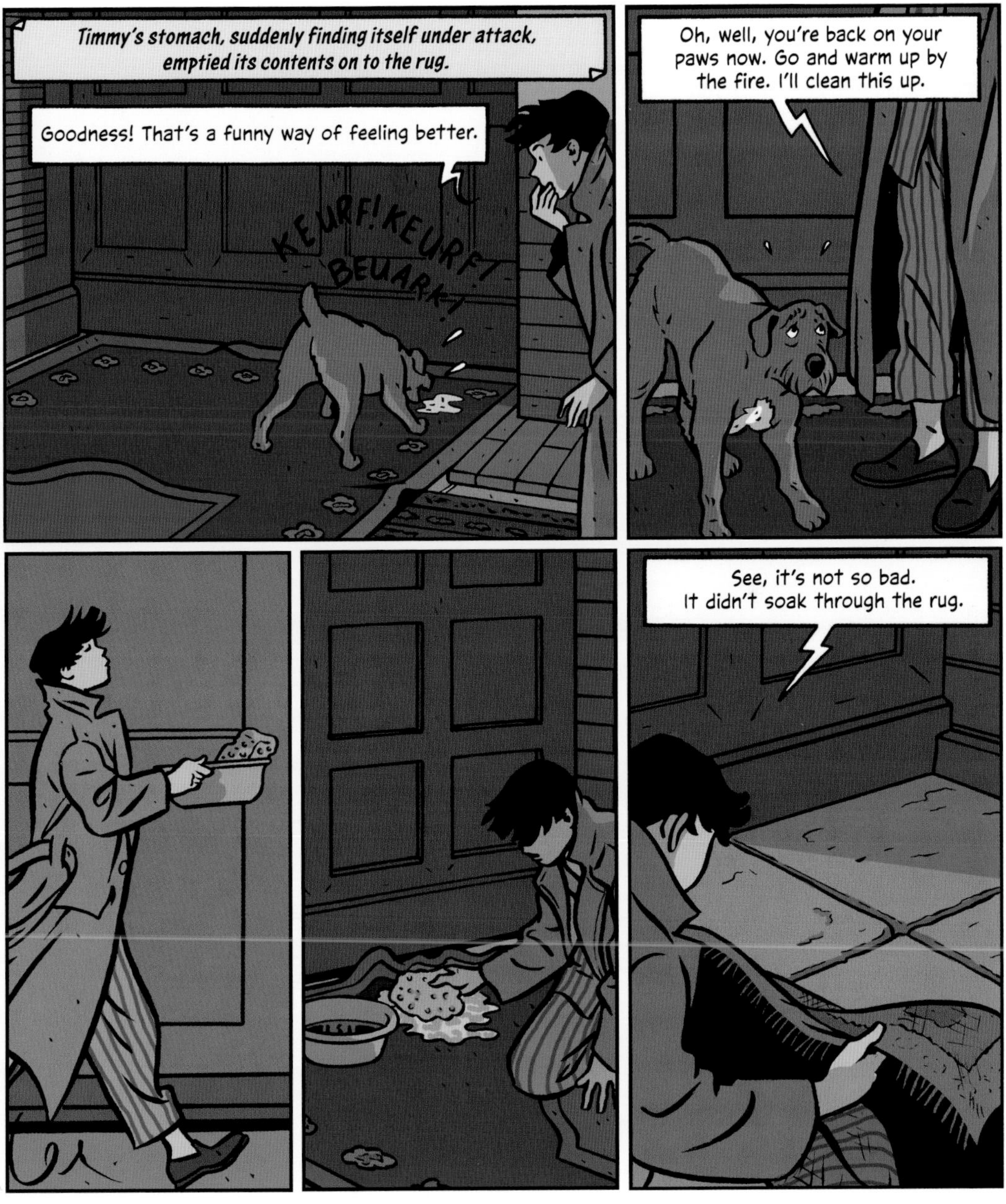

Timmy's stomach, suddenly finding itself under attack, emptied its contents on to the rug.
Goodness! That's a funny way of feeling better.
KEURF! KEURF! BEUARK!
Oh, well, you're back on your paws now. Go and warm up by the fire. I'll clean this up.
See, it's not so bad. It didn't soak through the rug.

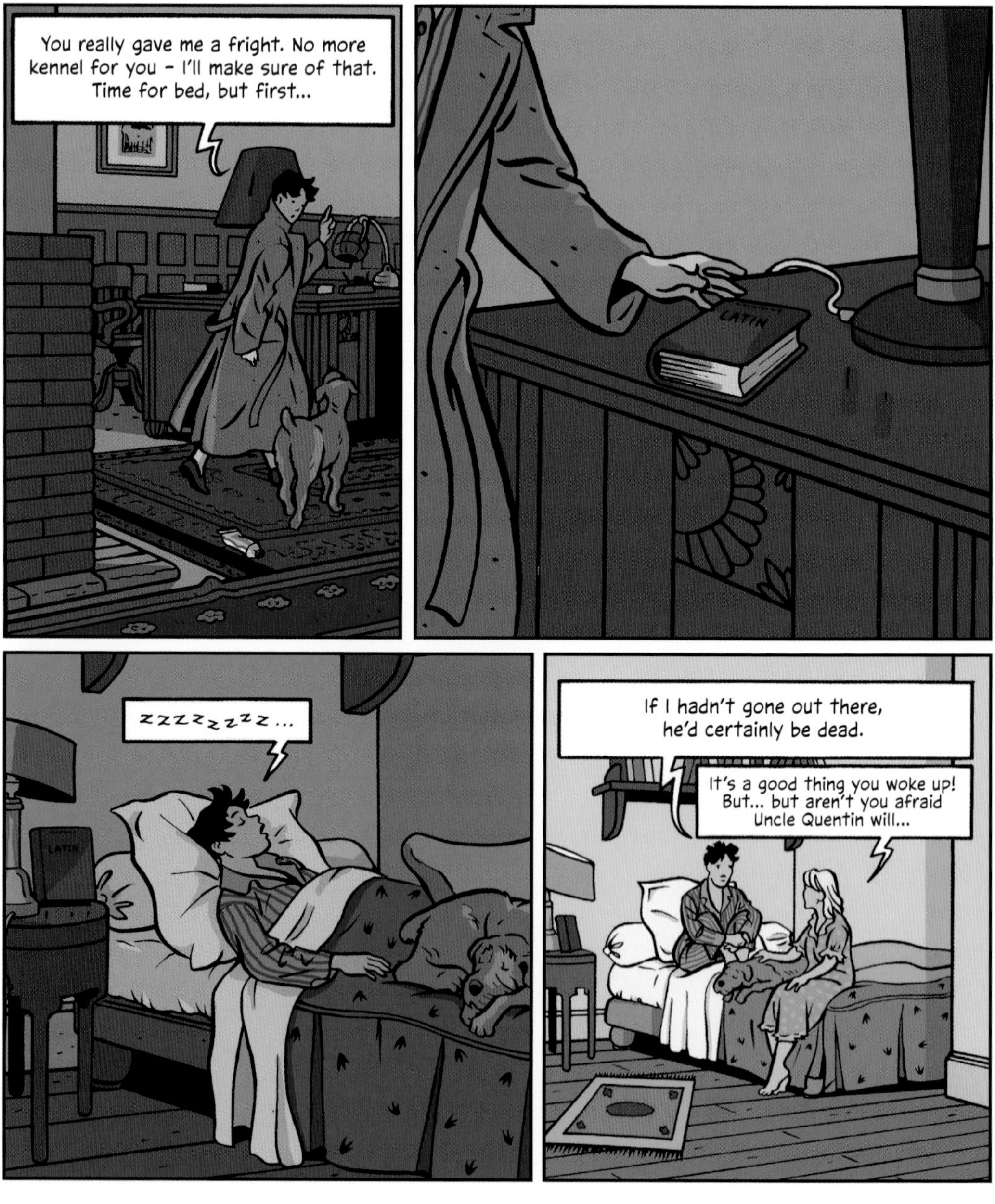
You really gave me a fright. No more kennel for you – I'll make sure of that. Time for bed, but first...
LATIN
LATIN
ZZZZZZZZ...
If I hadn't gone out there, he'd certainly be dead.
It's a good thing you woke up! But... but aren't you afraid Uncle Quentin will...

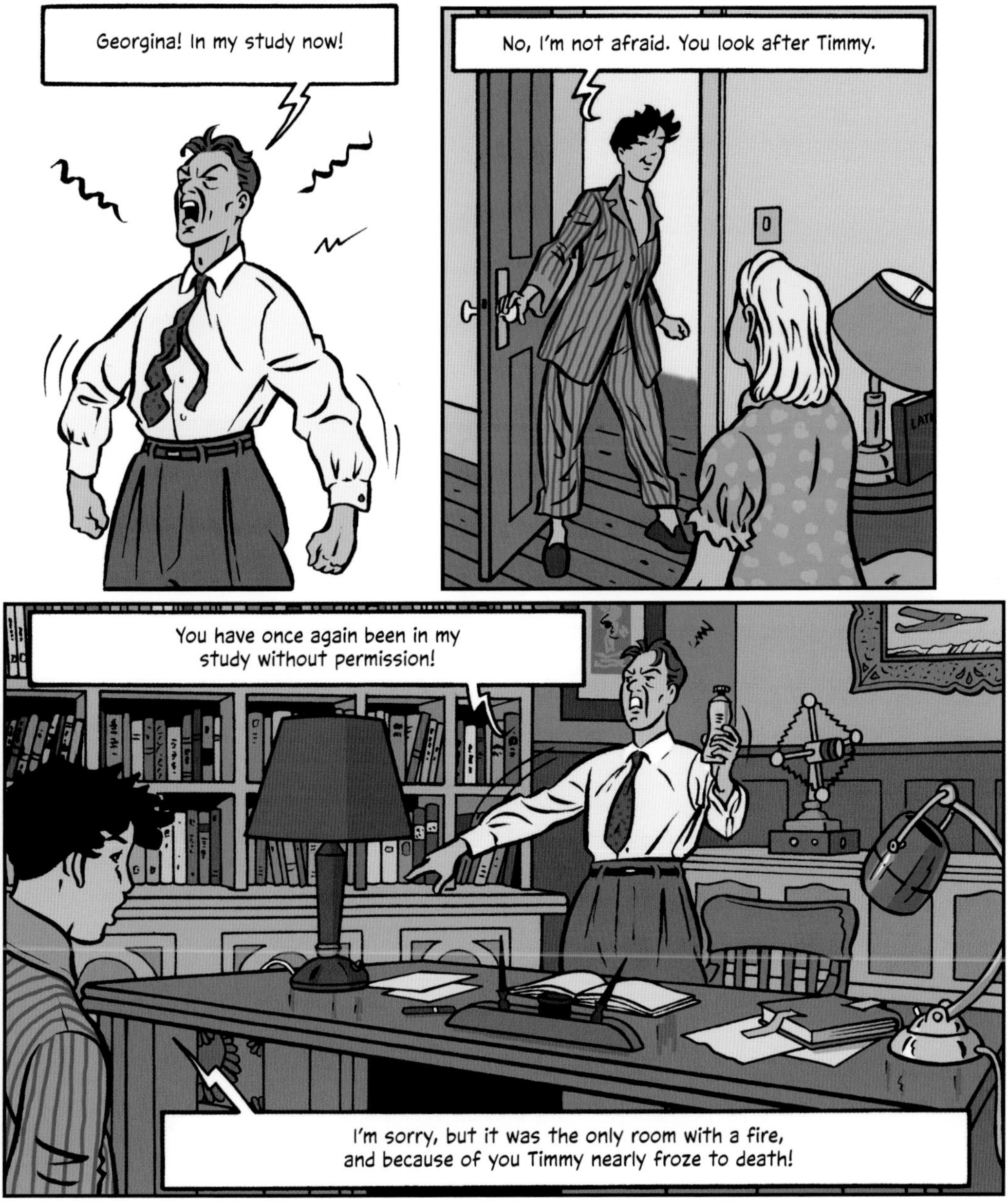
Georgina! In my study now!
No, I'm not afraid. You look after Timmy.
You have once again been in my study without permission!
I'm sorry, but it was the only room with a fire, and because of you Timmy nearly froze to death!

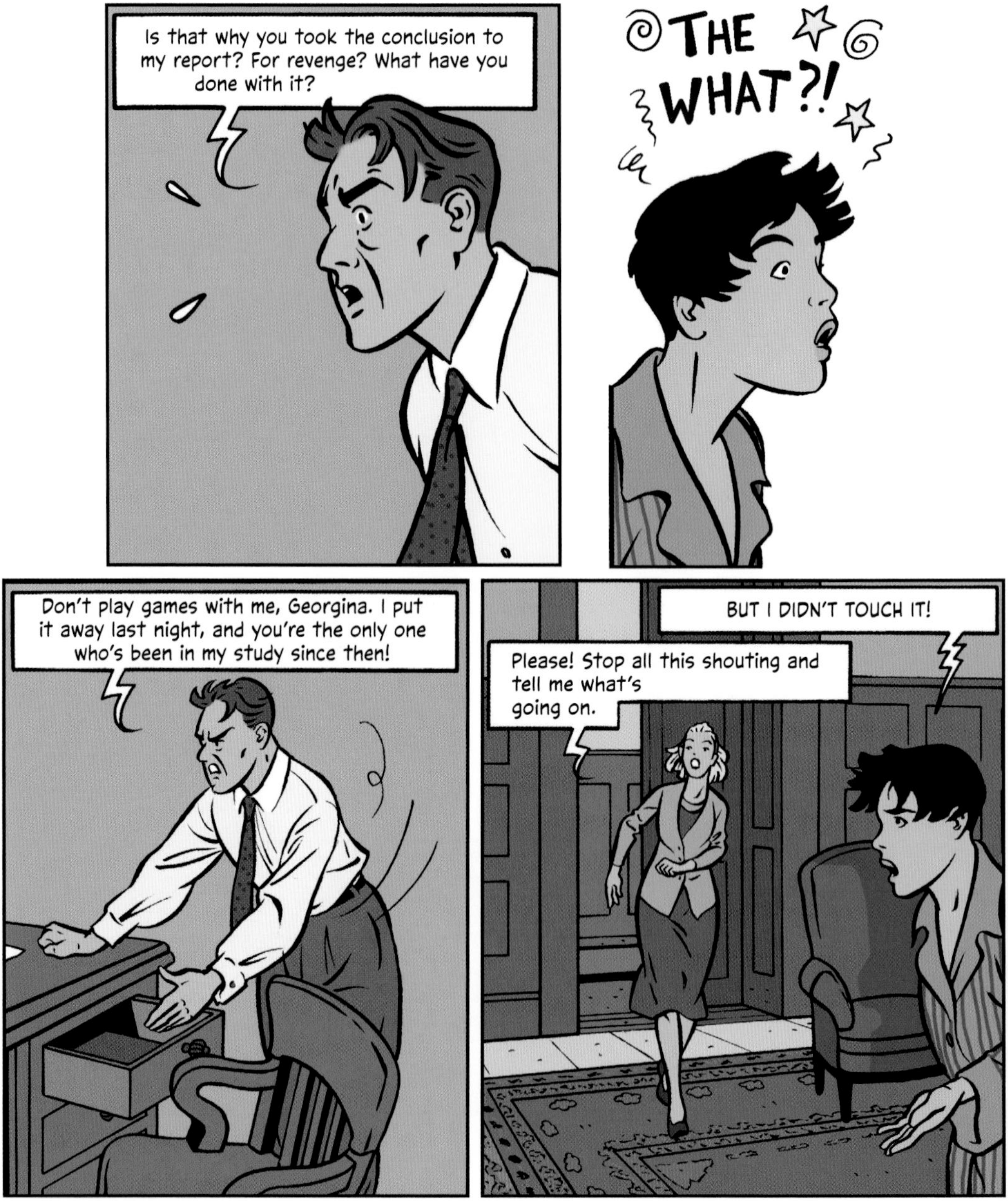
Is that why you took the conclusion to my report? For revenge? What have you done with it?
THE WHAT?!
Don't play games with me, Georgina. I put it away last night, and you're the only one who's been in my study since then!
BUT I DIDN'T TOUCH IT!
Please! Stop all this shouting and tell me what's going on.

Aunt Fanny, with her usual sweet and calming nature, managed to convince Uncle Quentin that George never lied. Nevertheless, after turning the study upside down, she had to admit that the documents were nowhere to be found.

George was absolutely certain that after she'd run to Timmy's rescue, the snow had stopped falling. Any thief entering the house from outside would have left footprints.

Anne and her brothers swore they'd been fast asleep. Their drowsy faces made it clear they were telling the truth.

By the time he had finished investigating, Uncle Quentin was nearly as upset by the unsolvable mystery as by the loss of his documents.

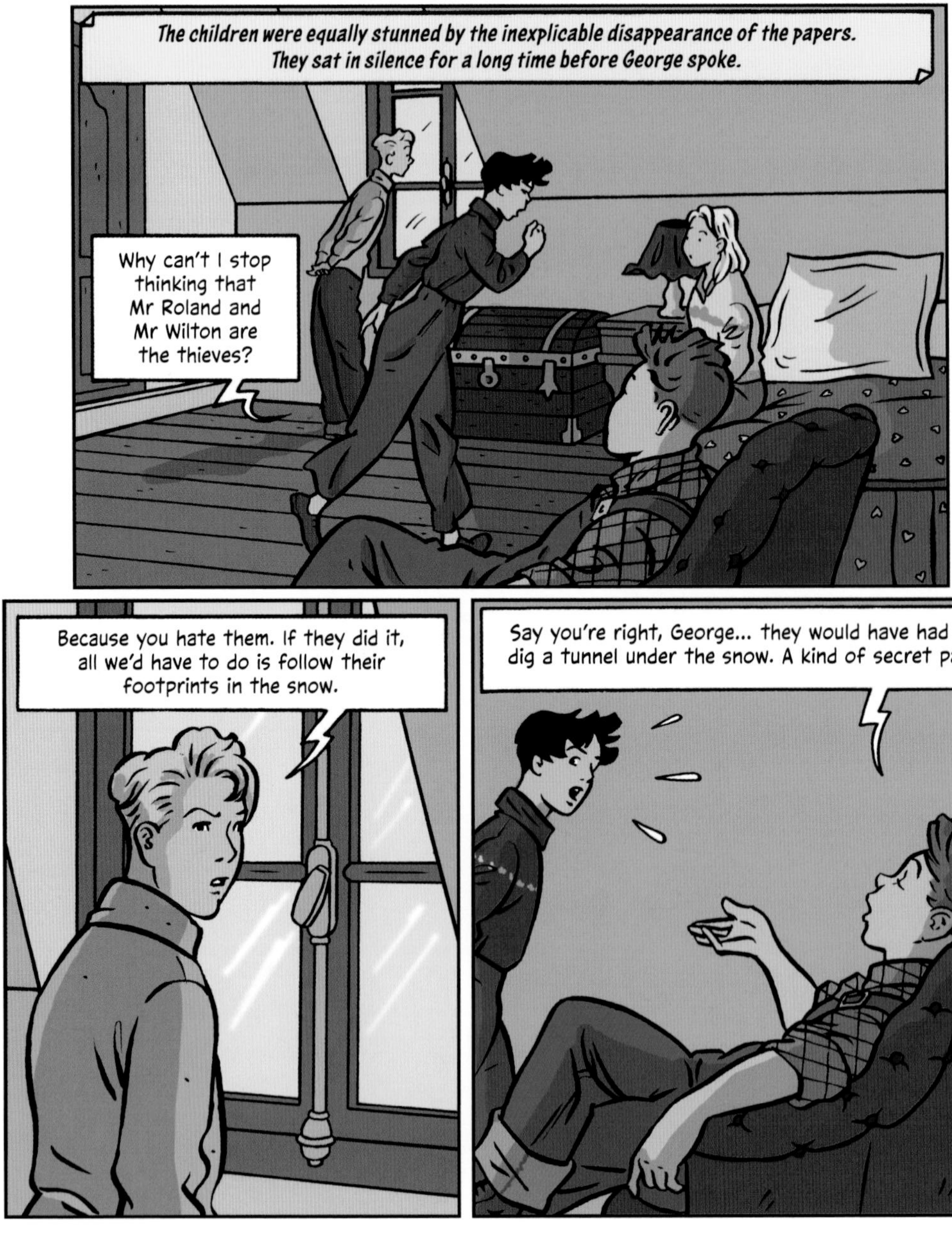
The children were equally stunned by the inexplicable disappearance of the papers. They sat in silence for a long time before George spoke.
Why can't I stop thinking that Mr Roland and Mr Wilton are the thieves?
Because you hate them. If they did it, all we'd have to do is follow their footprints in the snow.
Say you're right, George... they would have had to dig a tunnel under the snow. A kind of secret pa...

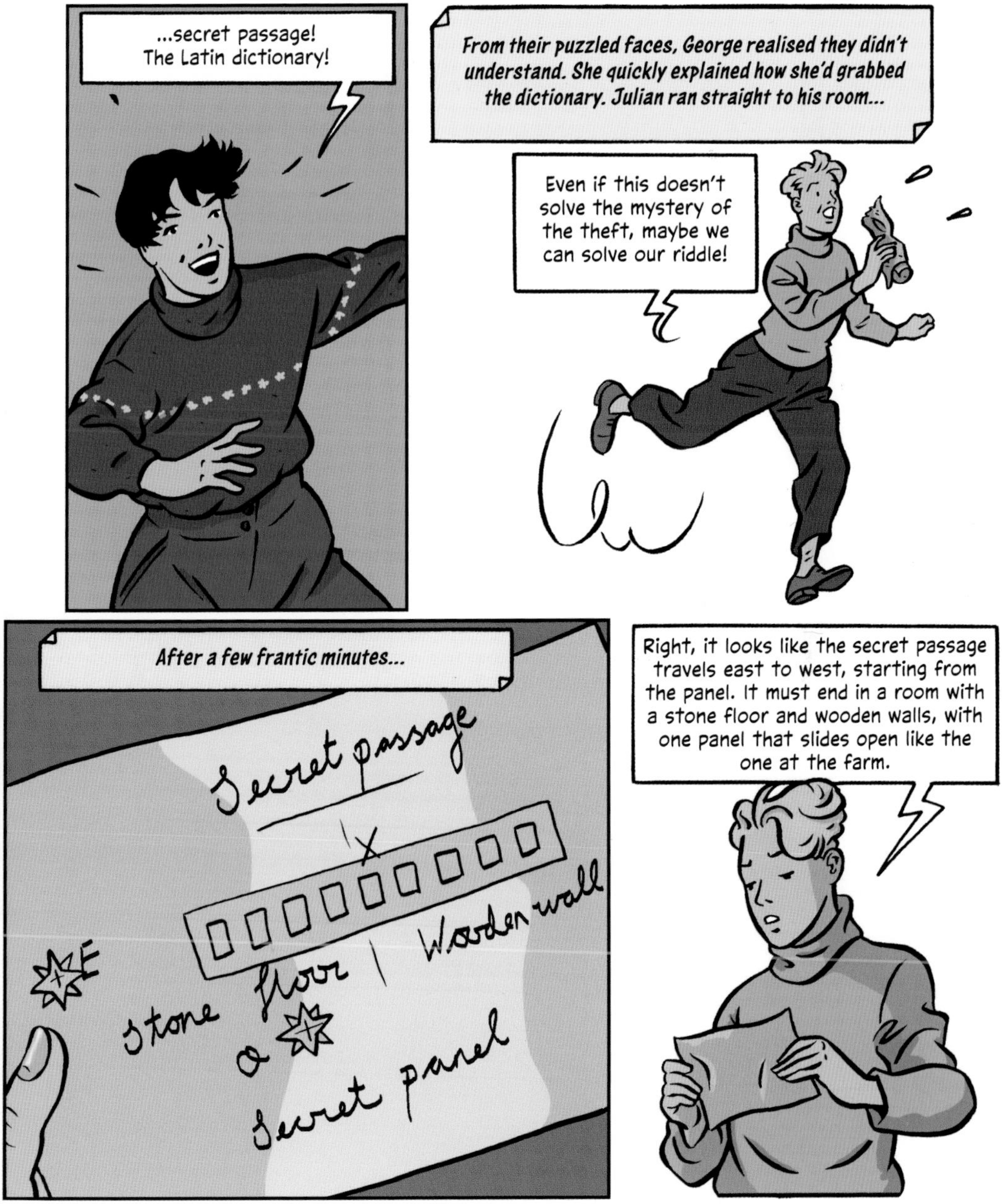
...secret passage! The Latin dictionary!
From their puzzled faces, George realised they didn't understand. She quickly explained how she'd grabbed the dictionary. Julian ran straight to his room...
Even if this doesn't solve the mystery of the theft, maybe we can solve our riddle!
After a few frantic minutes...
Secret passage
Wooden wall
E
Stone floor
Secret panel
Right, it looks like the secret passage travels east to west, starting from the panel. It must end in a room with a stone floor and wooden walls, with one panel that slides open like the one at the farm.

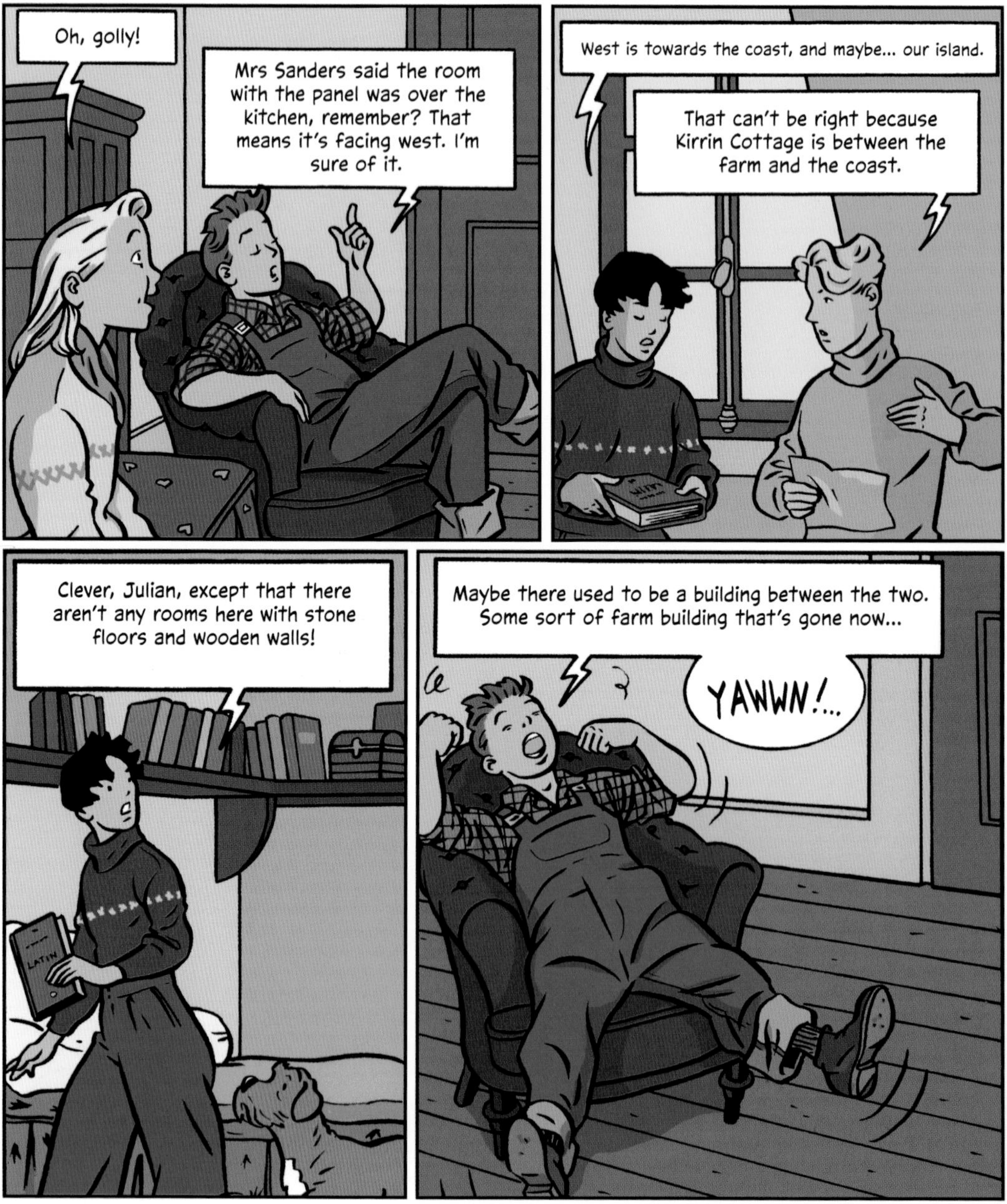

Oh, golly!
Mrs Sanders said the room with the panel was over the kitchen, remember? That means it's facing west. I'm sure of it.
West is towards the coast, and maybe... our island.
That can't be right because Kirrin Cottage is between the farm and the coast.
Clever, Julian, except that there aren't any rooms here with stone floors and wooden walls!
Maybe there used to be a building between the two. Some sort of farm building that's gone now...
YAWWN!...

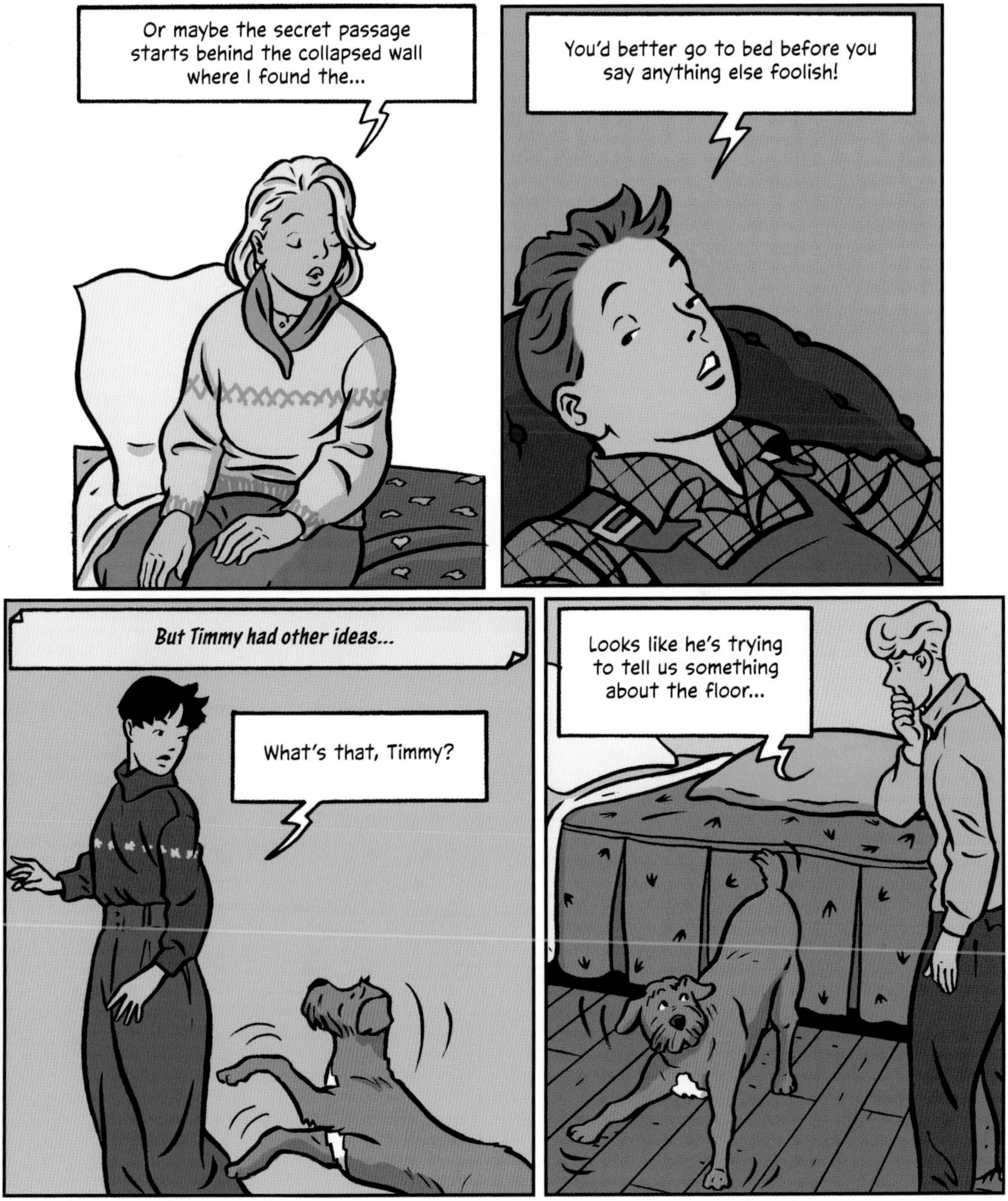
Or maybe the secret passage starts behind the collapsed wall where I found the...
You'd better go to bed before you say anything else foolish!
But Timmy had other ideas...
What's that, Timmy?
Looks like he's trying to tell us something about the floor...

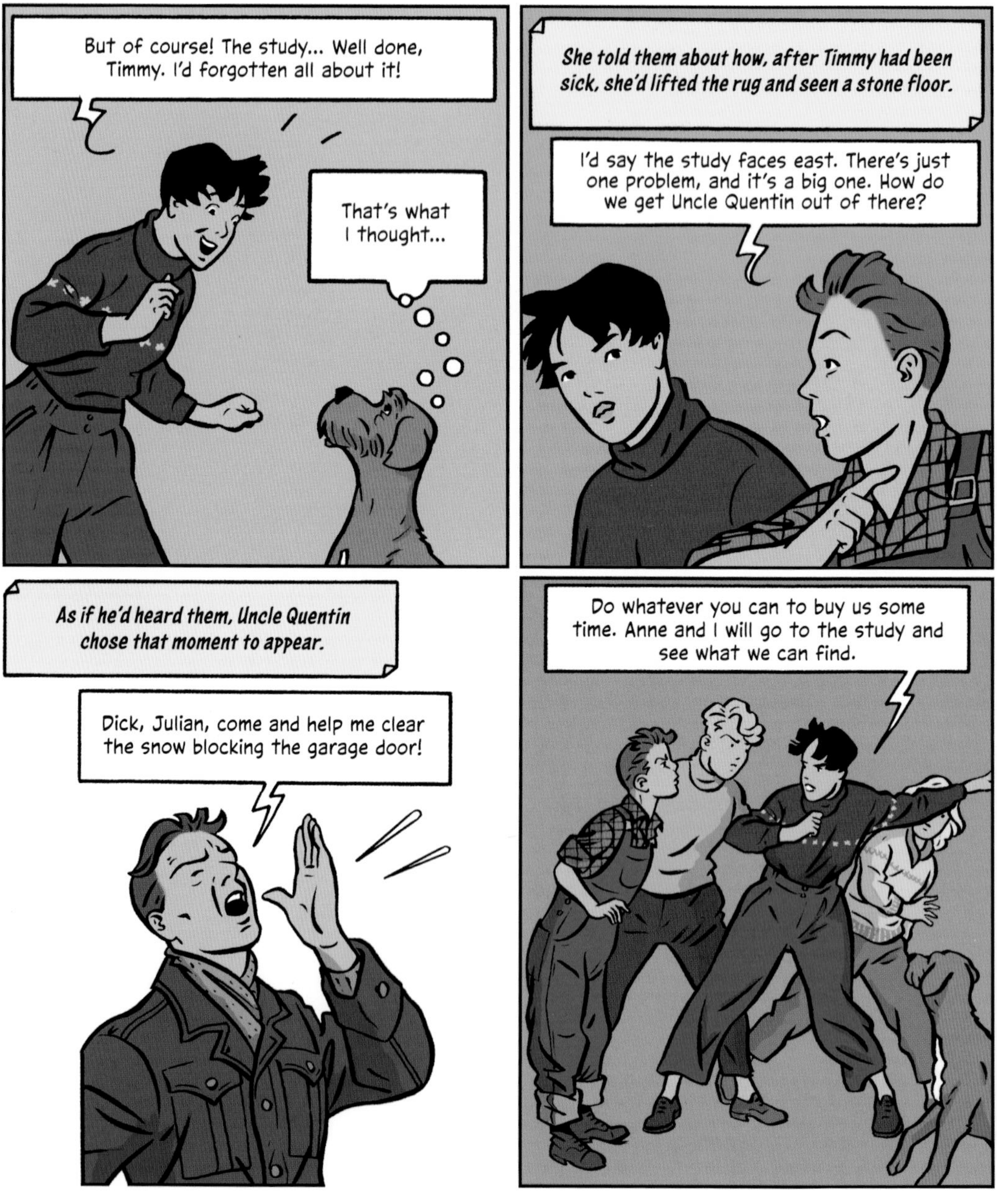

But of course! The study... Well done, Timmy. I'd forgotten all about it!
That's what I thought...
She told them about how, after Timmy had been sick, she'd lifted the rug and seen a stone floor.
I'd say the study faces east. There's just one problem, and it's a big one. How do we get Uncle Quentin out of there?
As if he'd heard them, Uncle Quentin chose that moment to appear.
Dick, Julian, come and help me clear the snow blocking the garage door!
Do whatever you can to buy us some time. Anne and I will go to the study and see what we can find.

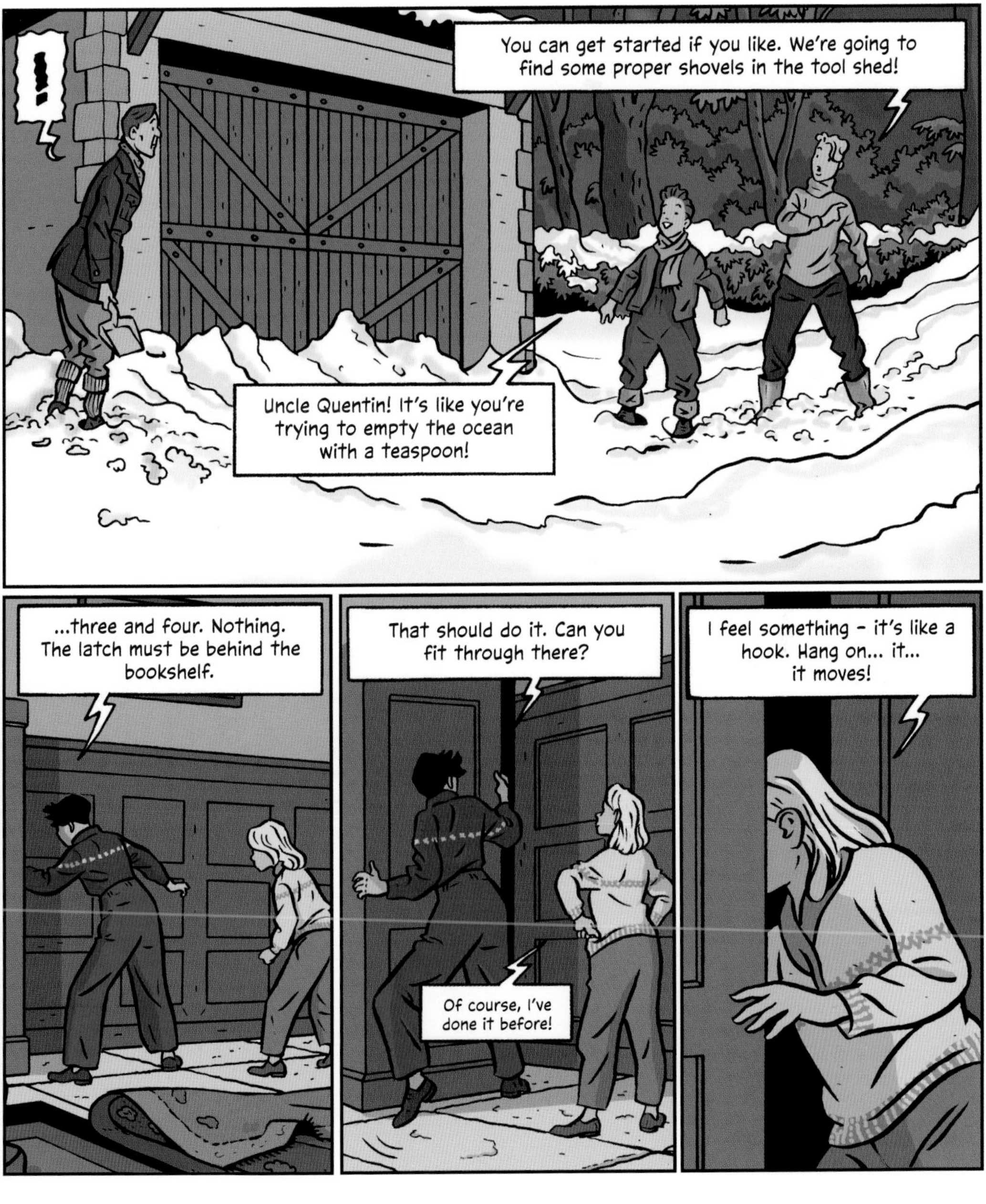
!
You can get started if you like. We're going to find some proper shovels in the tool shed!
Uncle Quentin! It's like you're trying to empty the ocean with a teaspoon!
...three and four. Nothing. The latch must be behind the bookshelf.
That should do it. Can you fit through there?
Of course, I've done it before!
I feel something – it's like a hook. Hang on... it... it moves!

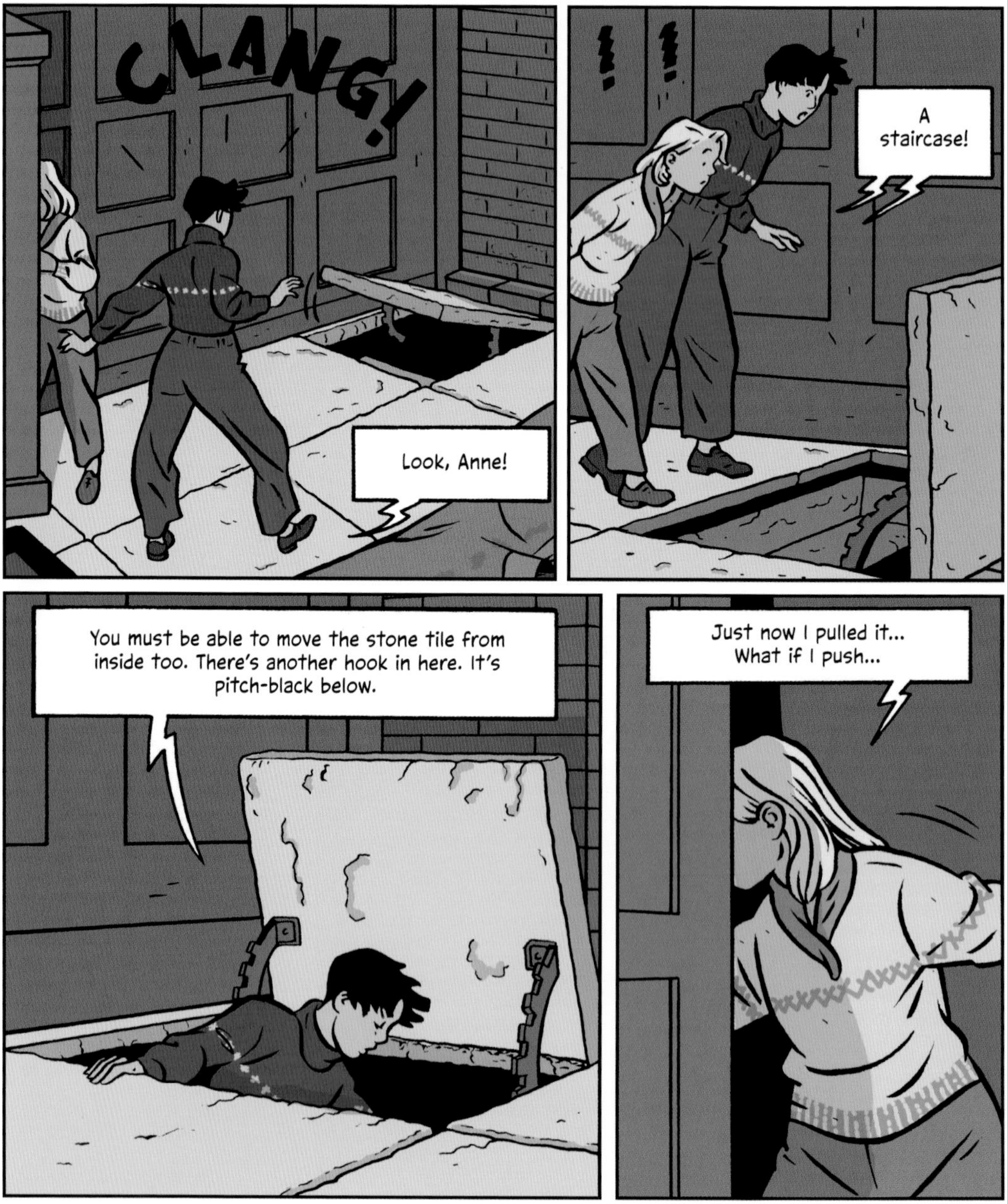
CLANG!
Look, Anne!
A staircase!
You must be able to move the stone tile from inside too. There's another hook in here. It's pitch-black below.
Just now I pulled it... What if I push...

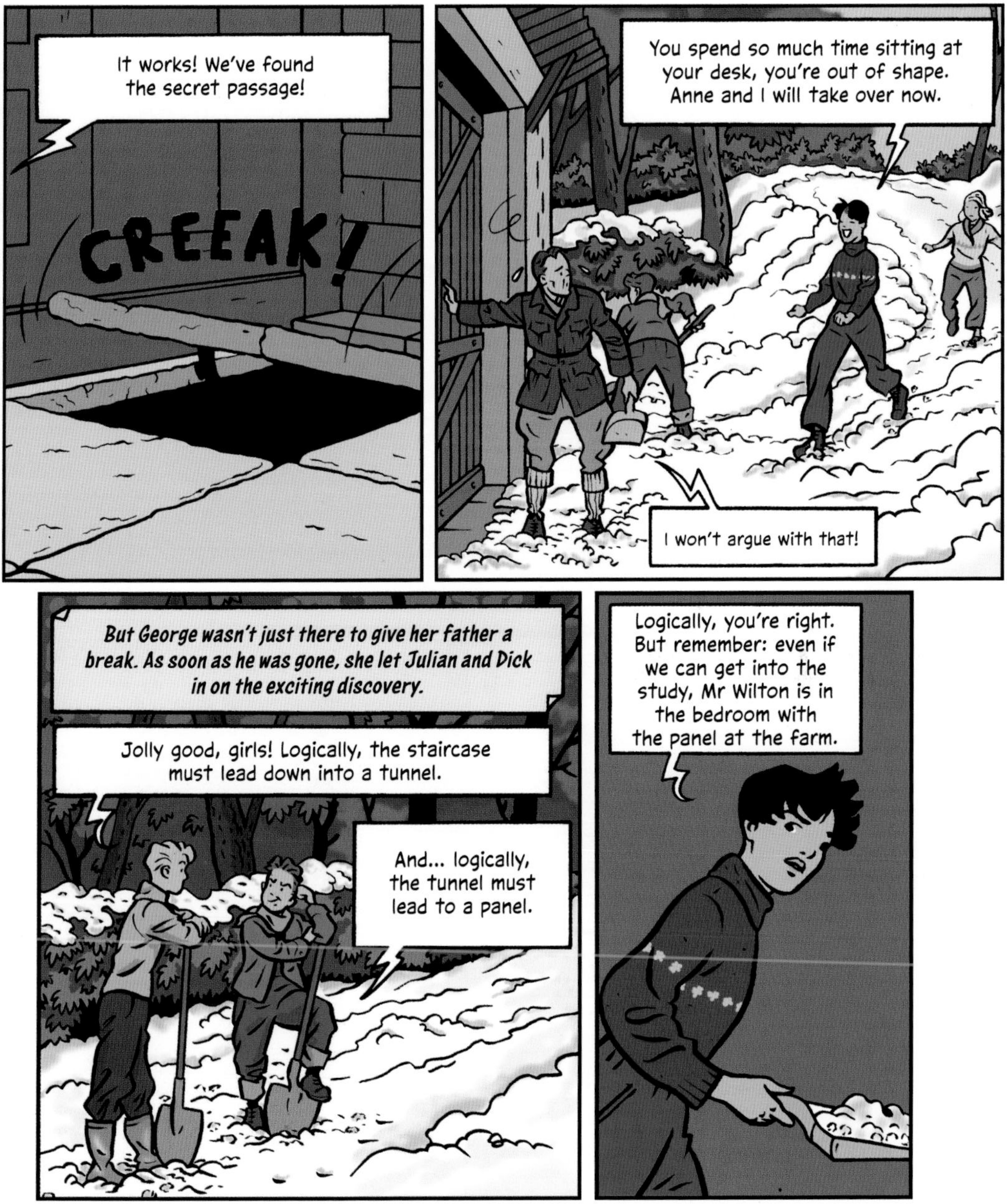

It works! We've found the secret passage!
CREEAK!
You spend so much time sitting at your desk, you're out of shape. Anne and I will take over now.
I won't argue with that!
But George wasn't just there to give her father a break. As soon as he was gone, she let Julian and Dick in on the exciting discovery.
Jolly good, girls! Logically, the staircase must lead down into a tunnel.
And... logically, the tunnel must lead to a panel.
Logically, you're right. But remember: even if we can get into the study, Mr Wilton is in the bedroom with the panel at the farm.

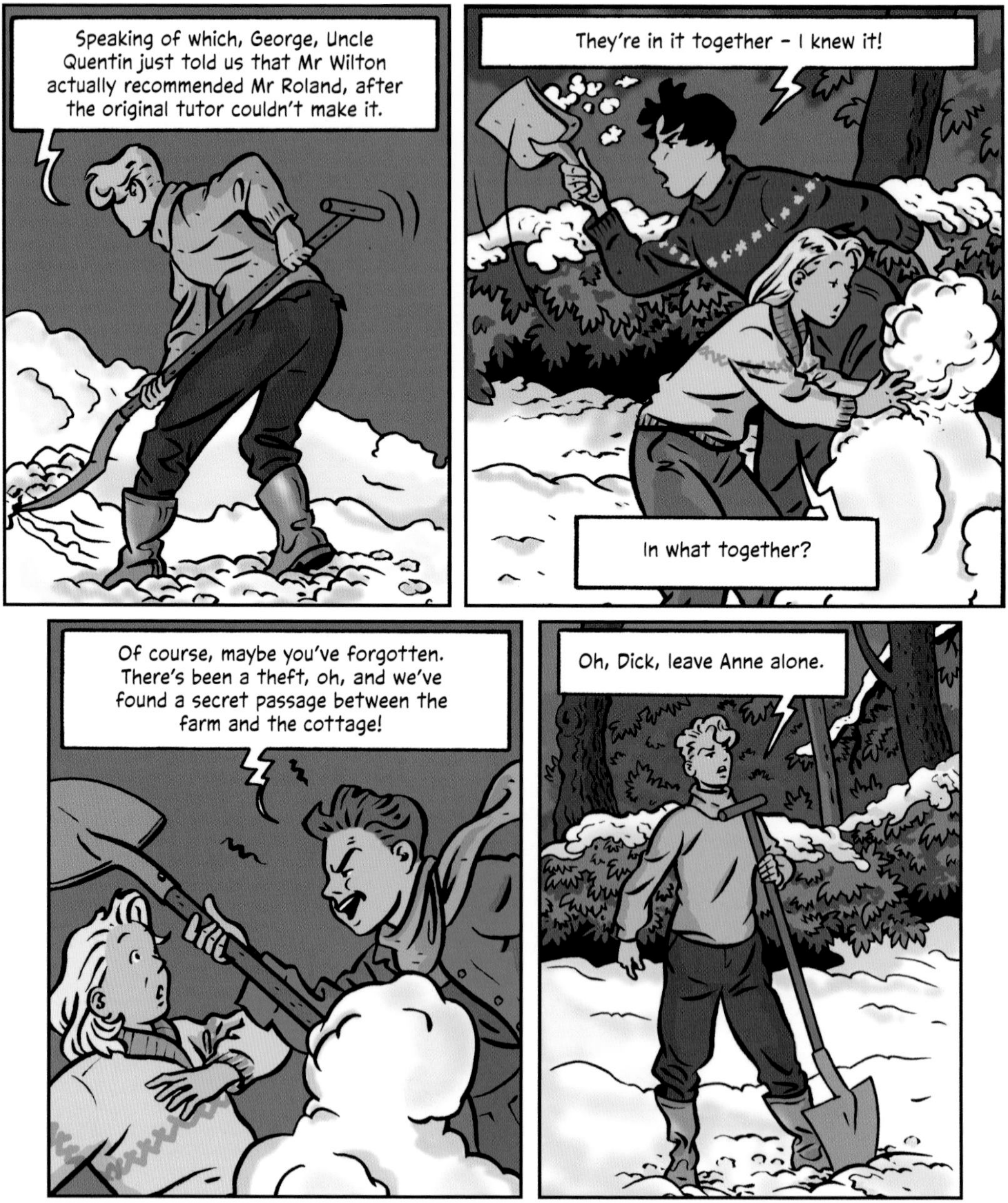
Speaking of which, George, Uncle Quentin just told us that Mr Wilton actually recommended Mr Roland, after the original tutor couldn't make it.
They're in it together – I knew it!
In what together?
Of course, maybe you've forgotten. There's been a theft, oh, and we've found a secret passage between the farm and the cottage!
Oh, Dick, leave Anne alone.

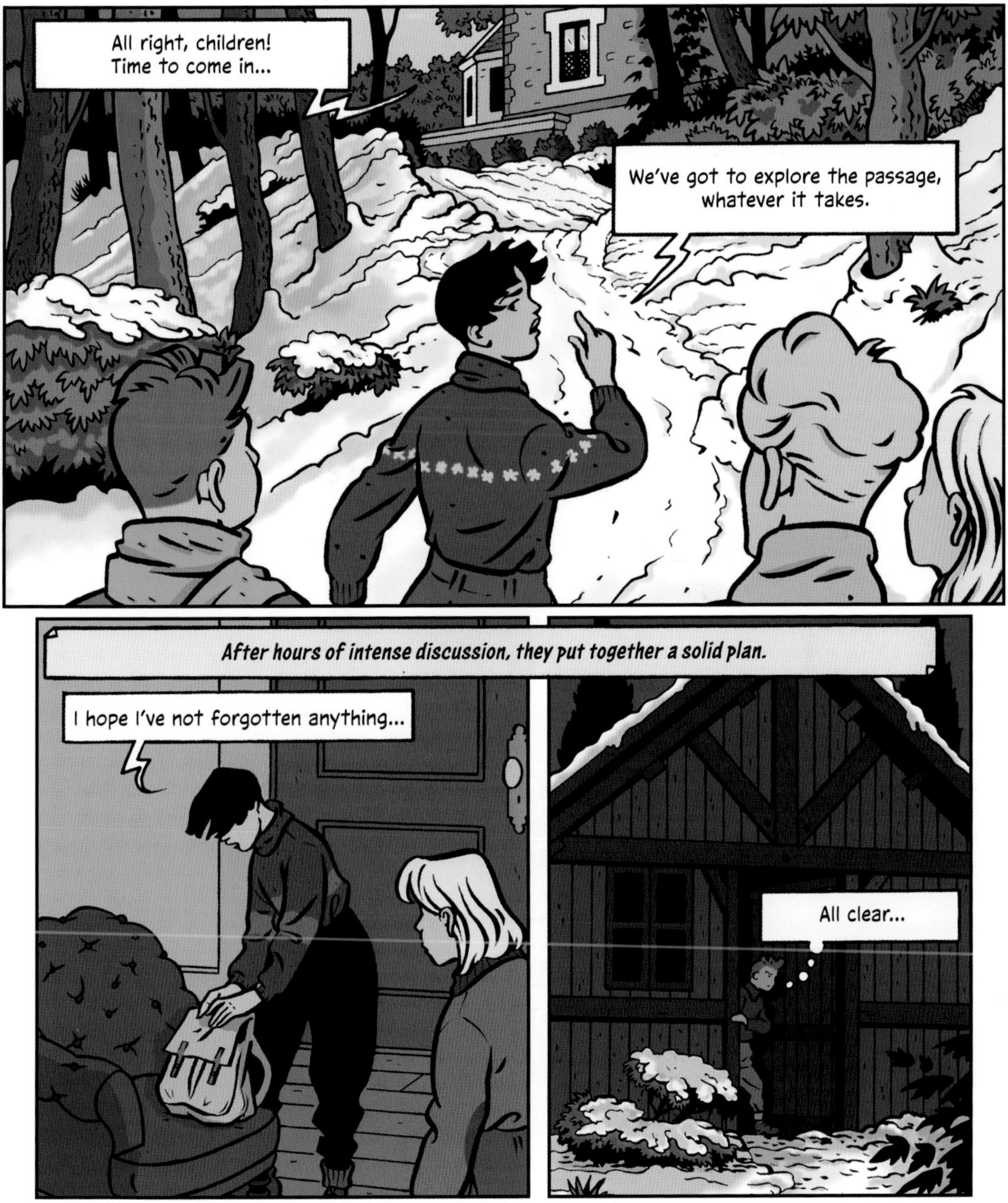
All right, children! Time to come in...
We've got to explore the passage, whatever it takes.
After hours of intense discussion, they put together a solid plan.
I hope I've not forgotten anything...
All clear...

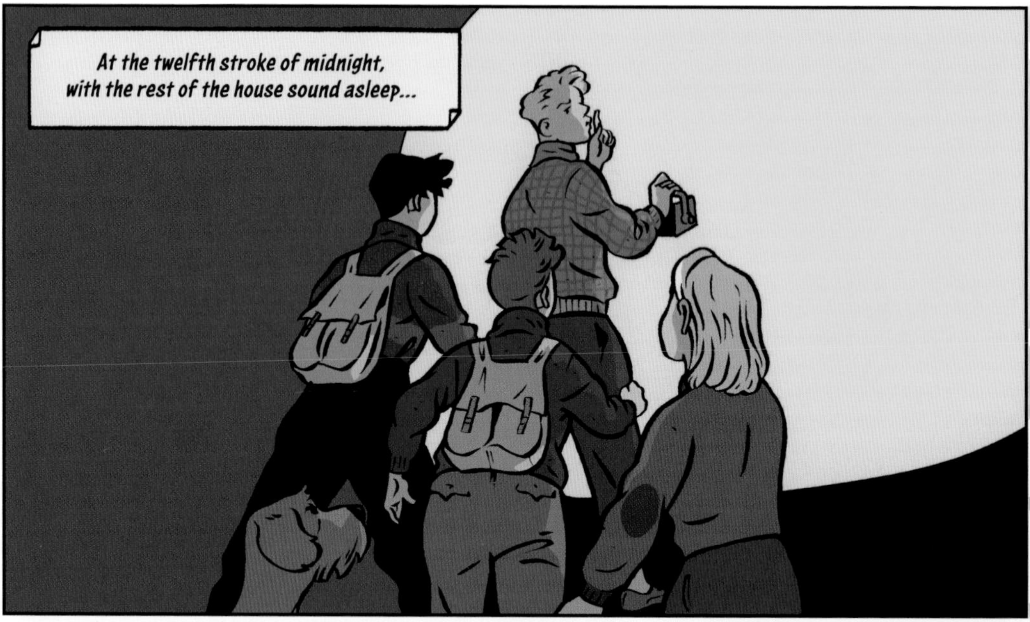
At the twelfth stroke of midnight,
with the rest of the house sound asleep...

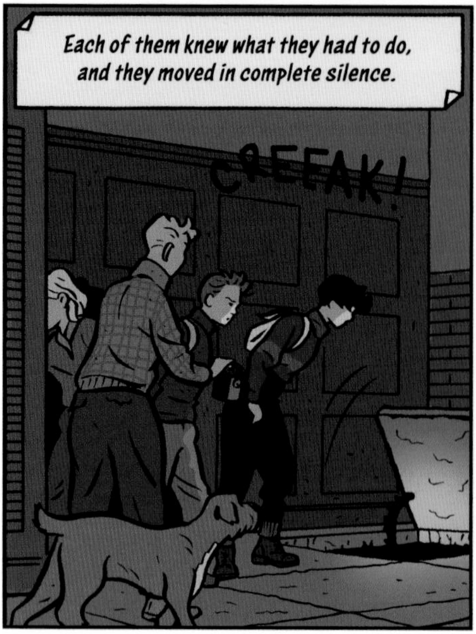
Each of them knew what they had to do,
and they moved in complete silence.
CREEAK!

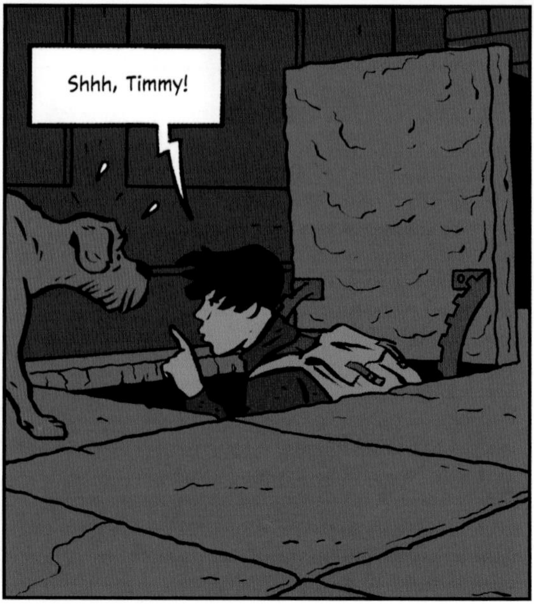
Shhh, Timmy!

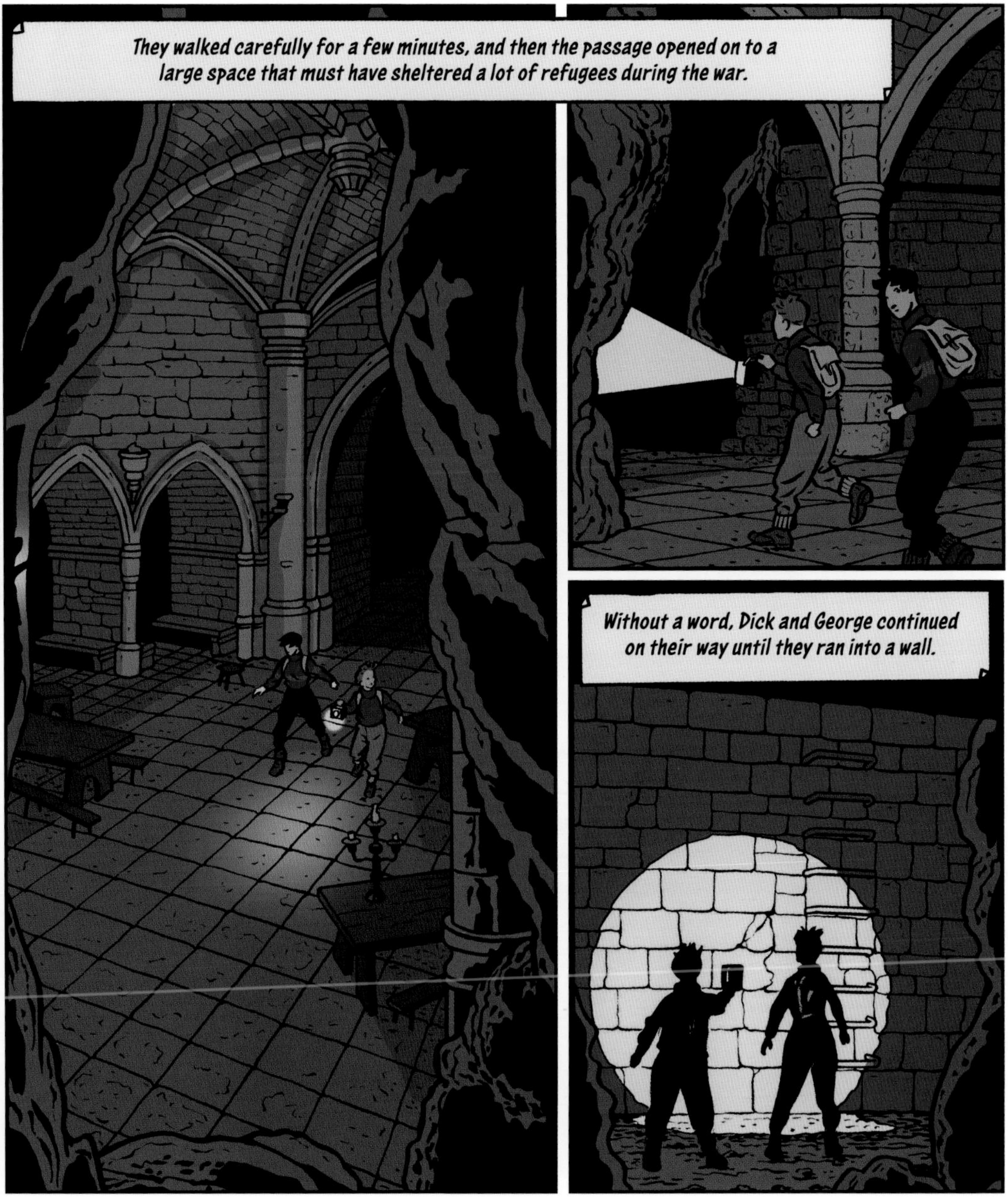
They walked carefully for a few minutes, and then the passage opened on to a large space that must have sheltered a lot of refugees during the war.
Without a word, Dick and George continued on their way until they ran into a wall.

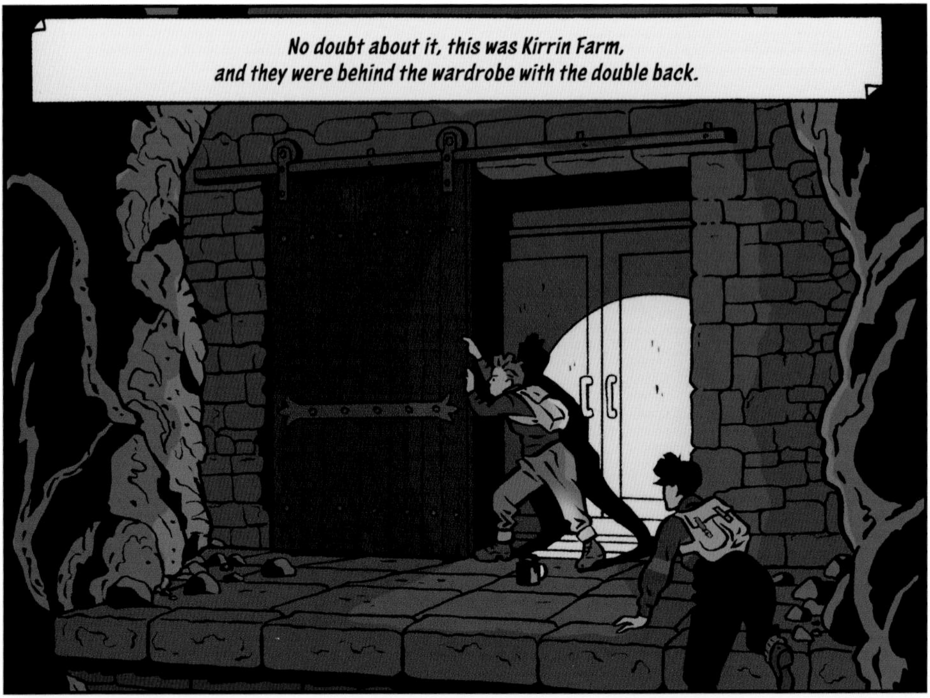
No doubt about it, this was Kirrin Farm, and they were behind the wardrobe with the double back.

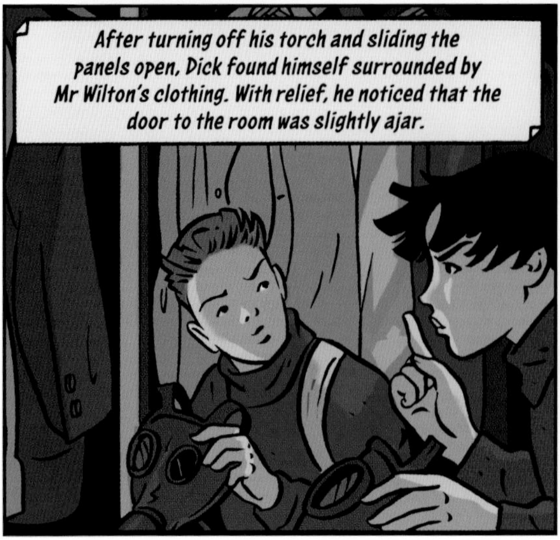
After turning off his torch and sliding the panels open, Dick found himself surrounded by Mr Wilton's clothing. With relief, he noticed that the door to the room was slightly ajar.

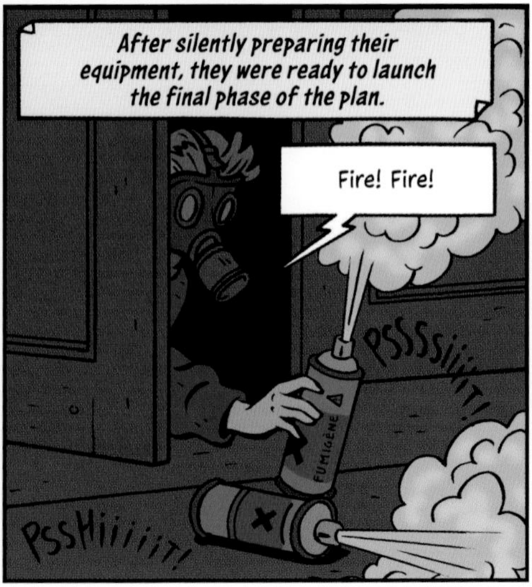
After silently preparing their equipment, they were ready to launch the final phase of the plan.
Fire! Fire!
PSSSsiiiiT!
FUMIGÈNE
PSSHiiiiiiT!

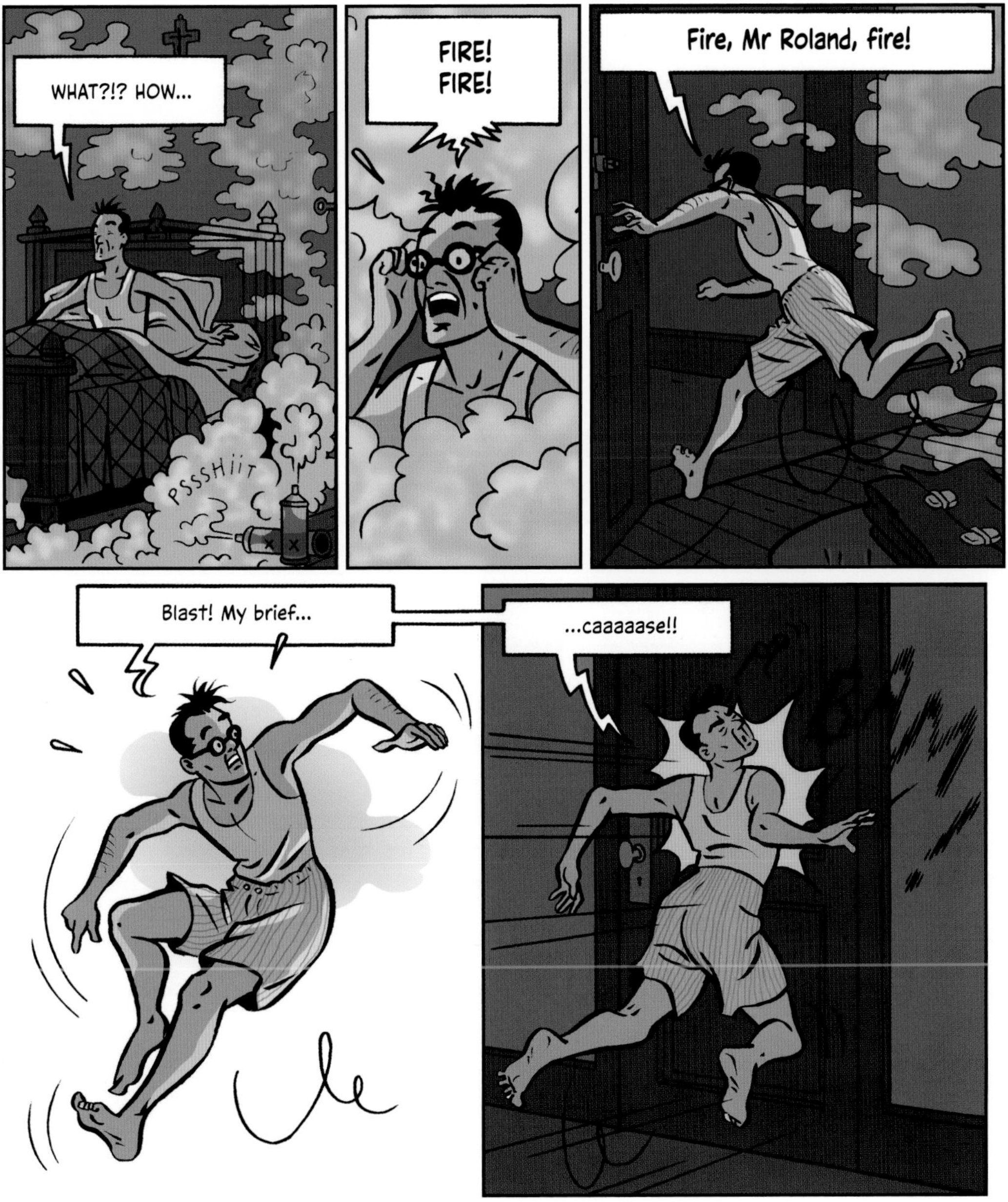
WHAT?!? HOW...
PSSSHiiT
FIRE!
FIRE!
Fire, Mr Roland, fire!
Blast! My brief...
...caaaaase!!

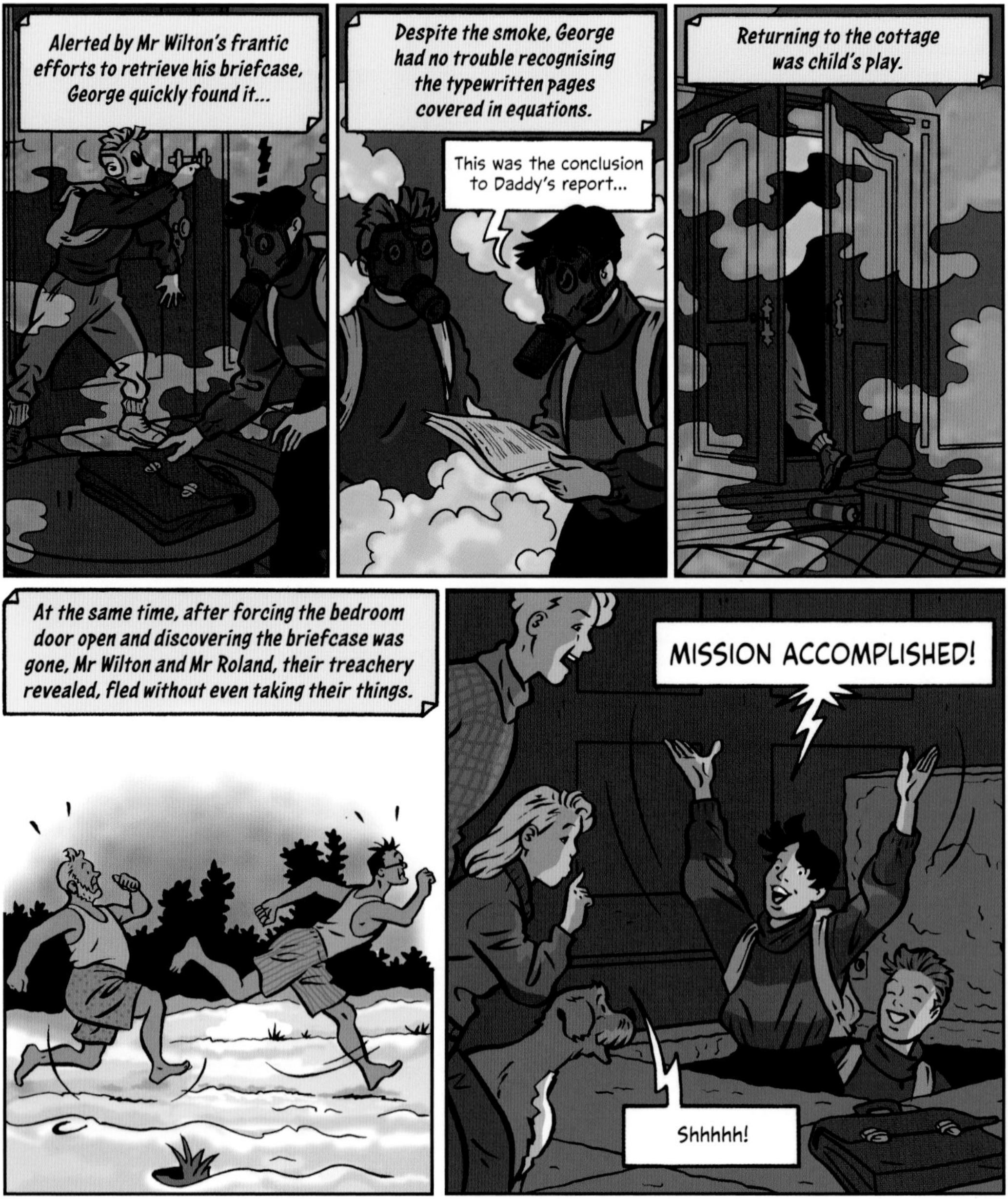

Alerted by Mr Wilton's frantic efforts to retrieve his briefcase, George quickly found it...
Despite the smoke, George had no trouble recognising the typewritten pages covered in equations.
This was the conclusion to Daddy's report...
Returning to the cottage was child's play.
At the same time, after forcing the bedroom door open and discovering the briefcase was gone, Mr Wilton and Mr Roland, their treachery revealed, fled without even taking their things.
MISSION ACCOMPLISHED!
Shhhhh!

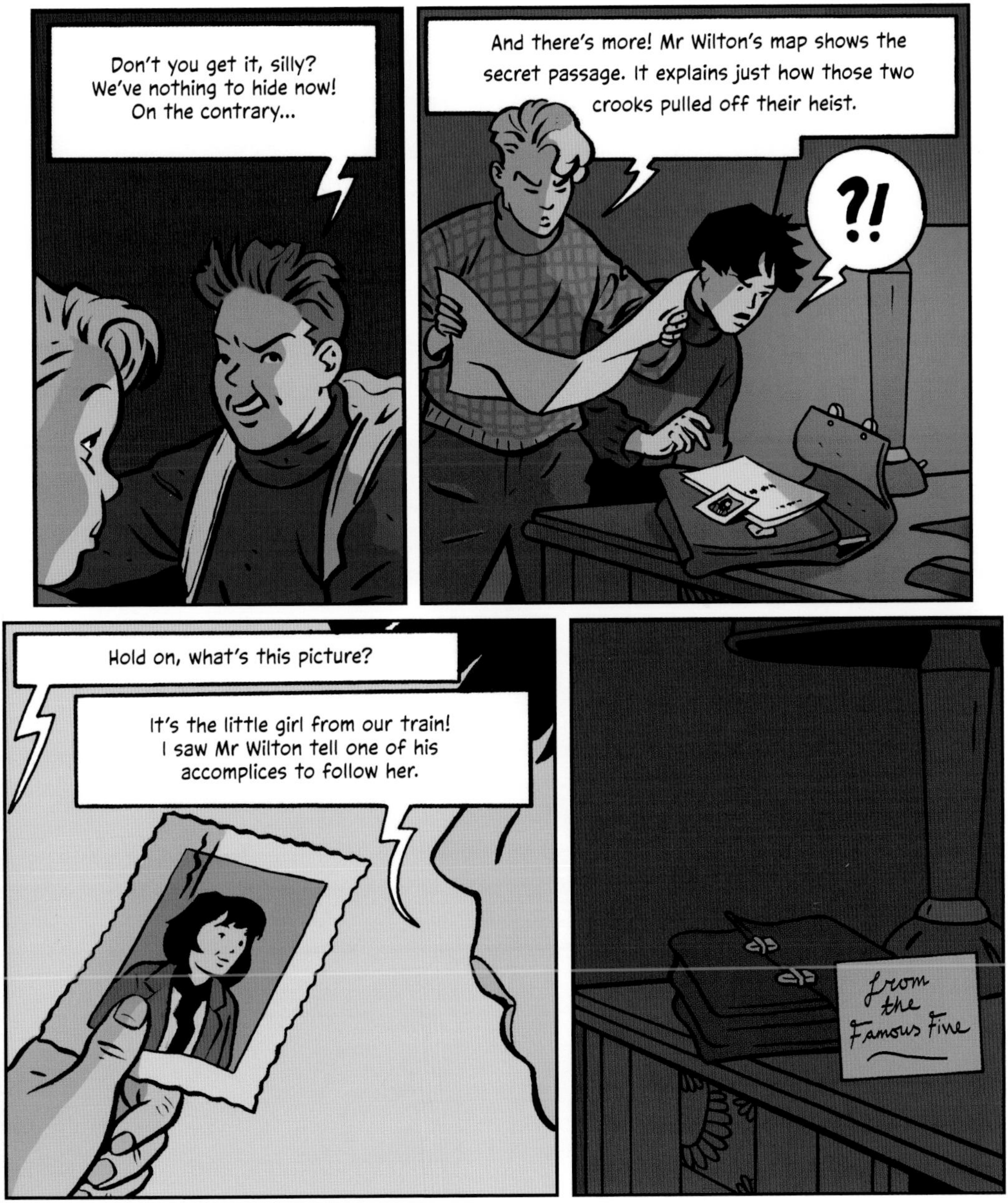
Don't you get it, silly?
We've nothing to hide now!
On the contrary...
And there's more! Mr Wilton's map shows the secret passage. It explains just how those two crooks pulled off their heist.
?!
Hold on, what's this picture?
It's the little girl from our train!
I saw Mr Wilton tell one of his
accomplices to follow her.
from the Famous Five

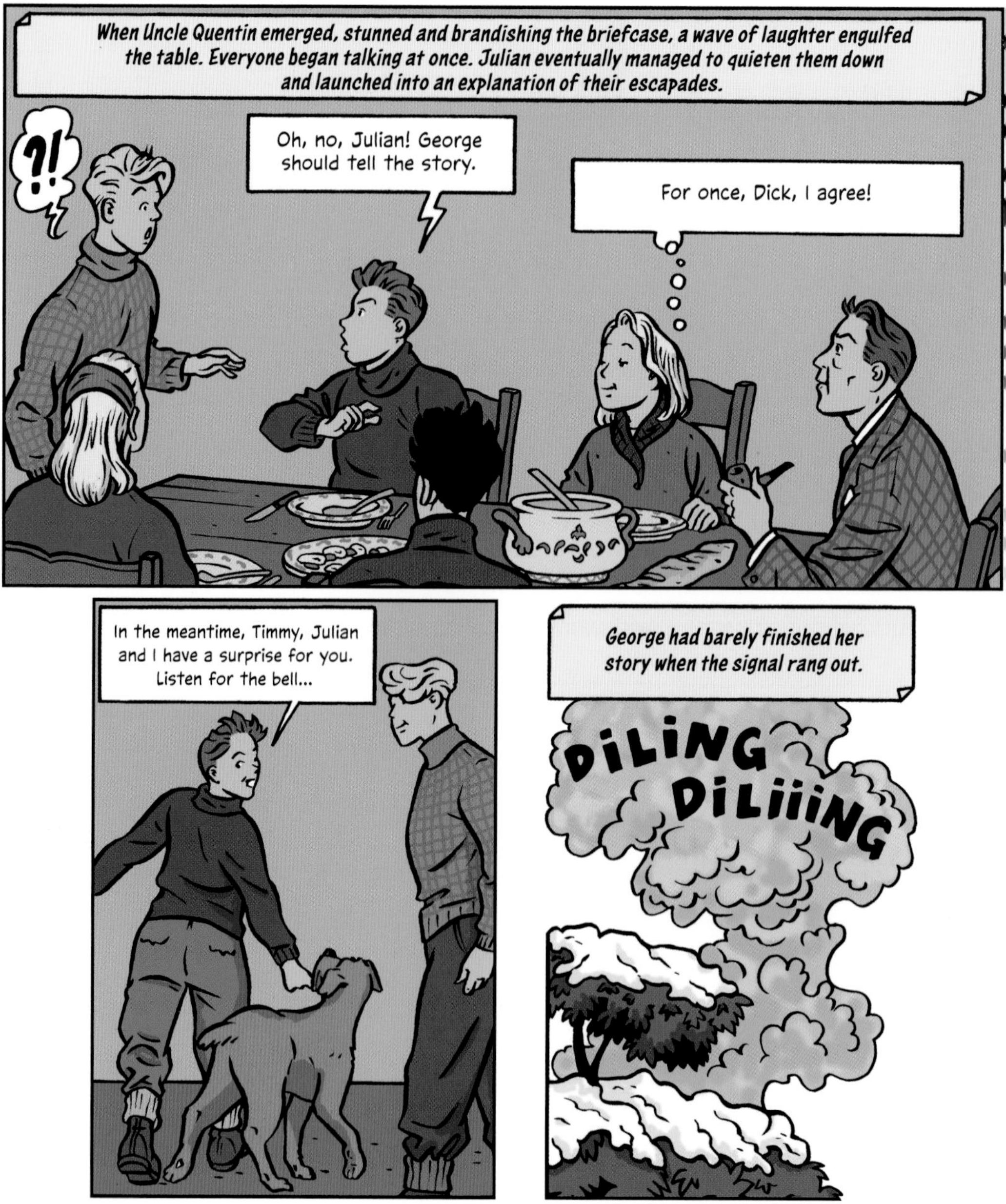
When Uncle Quentin emerged, stunned and brandishing the briefcase, a wave of laughter engulfed the table. Everyone began talking at once. Julian eventually managed to quieten them down and launched into an explanation of their escapades.
?!
Oh, no, Julian! George should tell the story.
For once, Dick, I agree!
In the meantime, Timmy, Julian and I have a surprise for you. Listen for the bell...
George had barely finished her story when the signal rang out.
DiLiNG
DiLiiiiNG

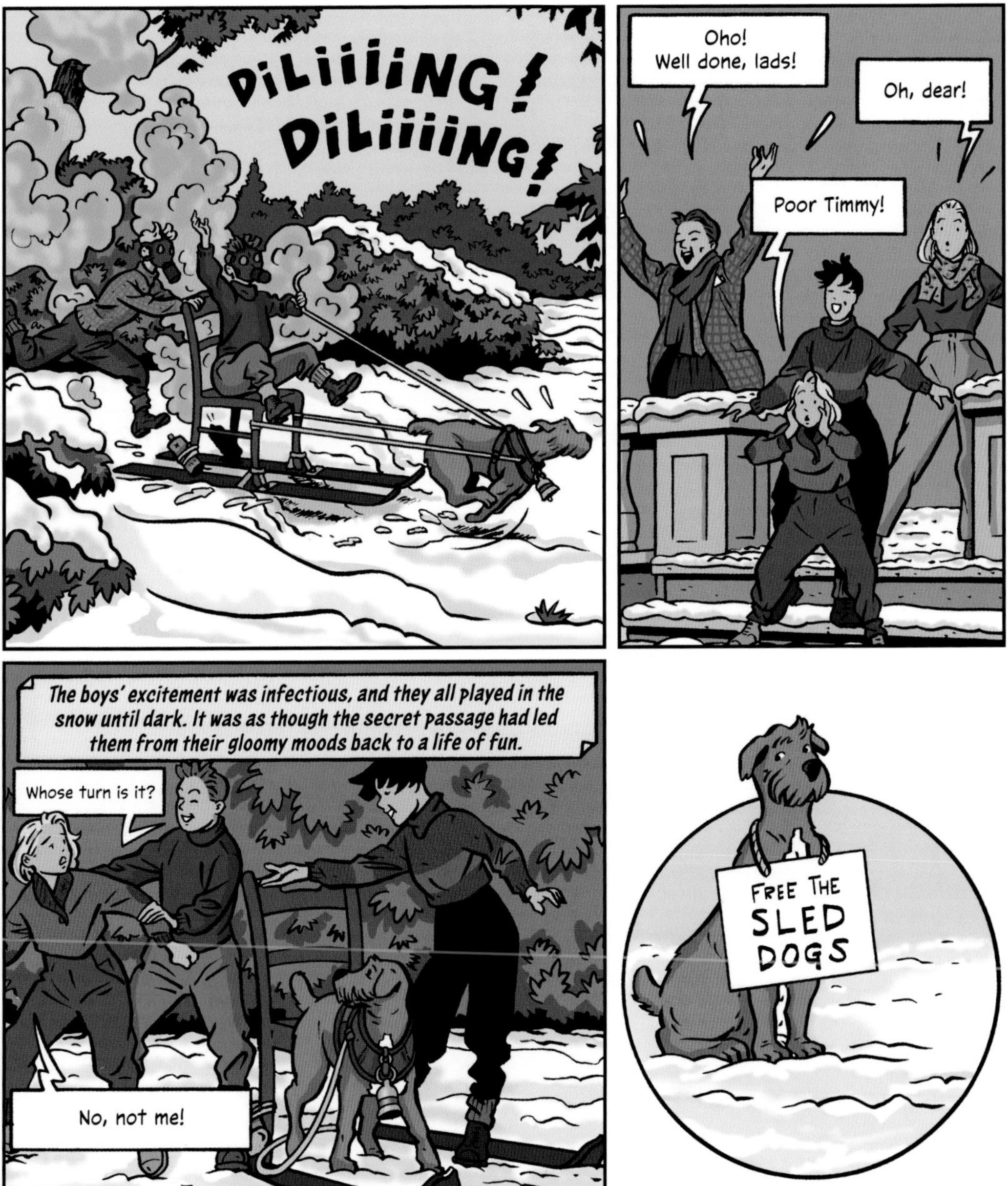
DILIIIING!
DILIIIING!
Oho!
Well done, lads!
Oh, dear!
Poor Timmy!
The boys' excitement was infectious, and they all played in the snow until dark. It was as though the secret passage had led them from their gloomy moods back to a life of fun.
Whose turn is it?
No, not me!
FREE THE SLED DOGS

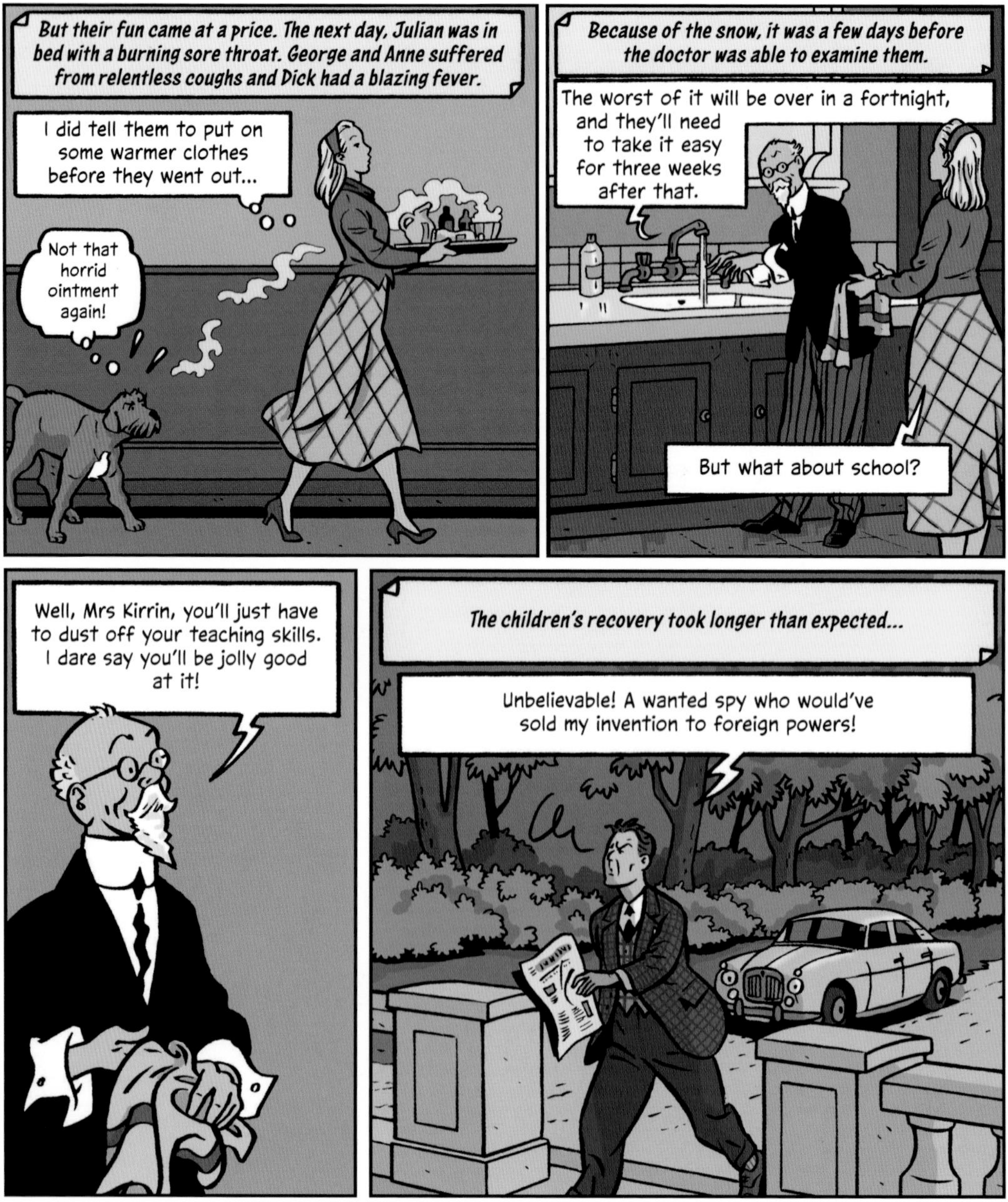
But their fun came at a price. The next day, Julian was in bed with a burning sore throat. George and Anne suffered from relentless coughs and Dick had a blazing fever.
I did tell them to put on some warmer clothes before they went out...
Not that horrid ointment again!
Because of the snow, it was a few days before the doctor was able to examine them.
The worst of it will be over in a fortnight, and they'll need to take it easy for three weeks after that.
But what about school?
Well, Mrs Kirrin, you'll just have to dust off your teaching skills. I dare say you'll be jolly good at it!
The children's recovery took longer than expected...
Unbelievable! A wanted spy who would've sold my invention to foreign powers!

CHILDREN, GATHER ROUND!

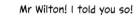

Mr Wilton! I told you so!

After a frantic stampede which attested to their newly recovered strength...

Look at this!

KIDNAPPING

Police are still seeking information on the whereabouts of Jennifer, missing for two weeks. The fugitive is suspected of kidnapping. one Mr Wilton by the police.

I've just come from the police station. They mentioned his spying but... not kidnapping! I hate to see such terrible crimes go unpunished!

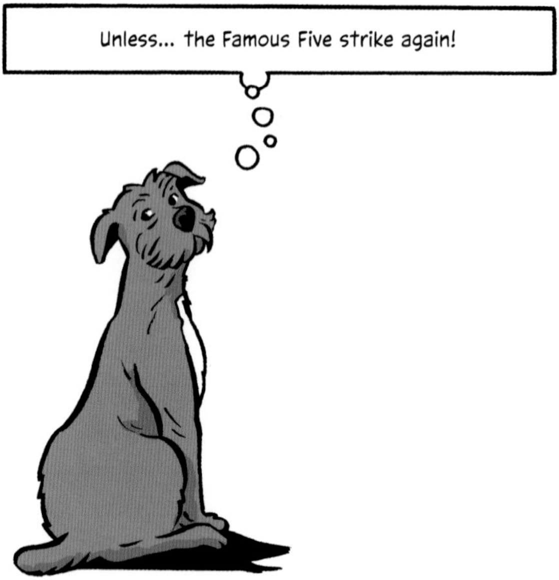
Unless... the Famous Five strike again!

The End

Join the Adventure

THE FAMOUS FIVE

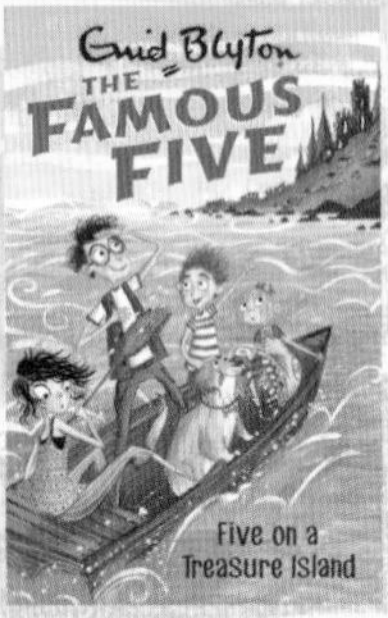
Enid Blyton
THE FAMOUS FIVE
Five on a Treasure Island

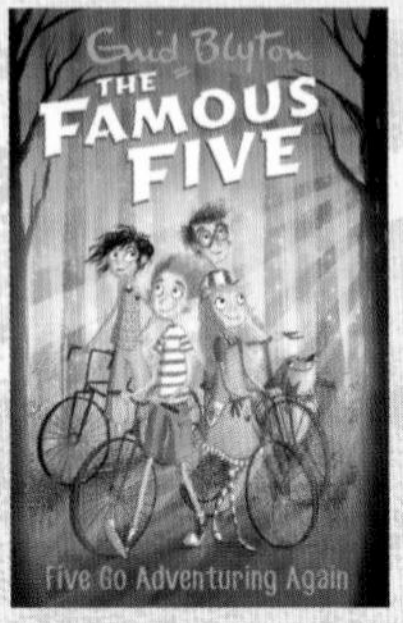
Enid Blyton
THE FAMOUS FIVE
Five Go Adventuring Again

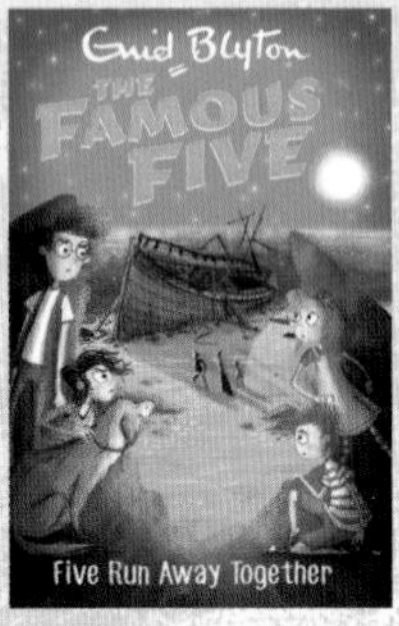
Enid Blyton
THE FAMOUS FIVE
Five Run Away Together

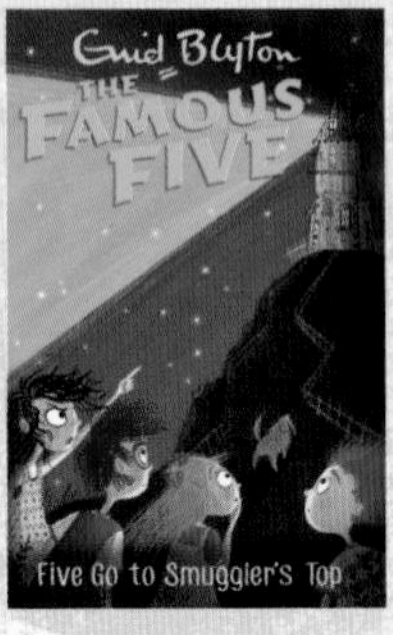
Enid Blyton
THE FAMOUS FIVE
Five Go to Smuggler's Top

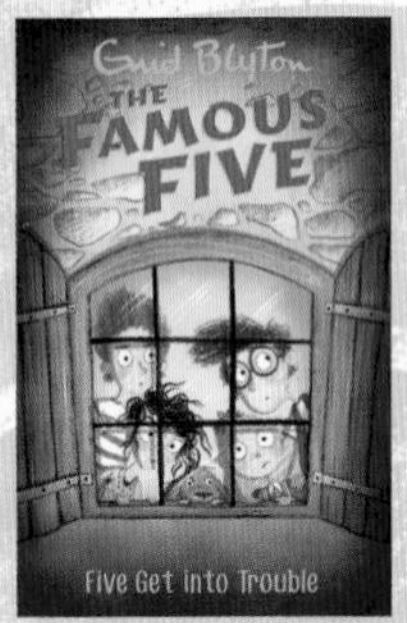
Enid Blyton
THE FAMOUS FIVE
Five Get into Trouble

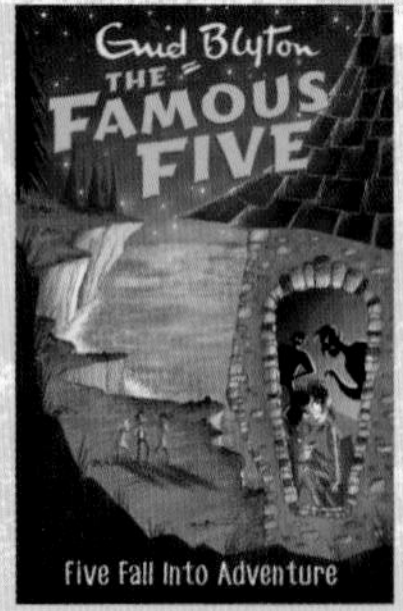
Enid Blyton
THE FAMOUS FIVE
Five Fall Into Adventure

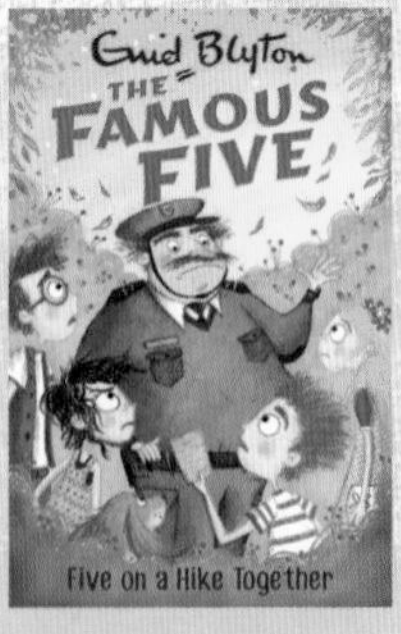
Enid Blyton
THE FAMOUS FIVE
Five on a Hike Together

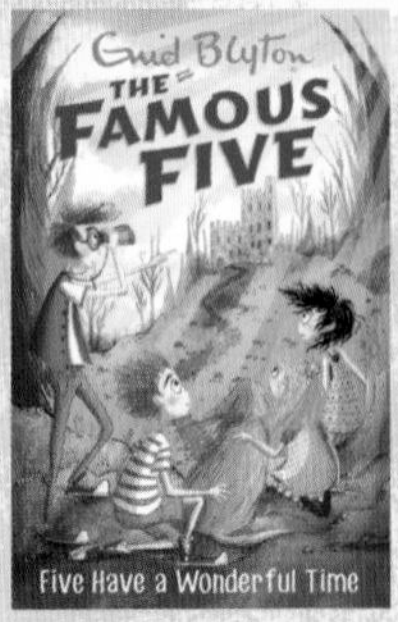
Enid Blyton
THE FAMOUS FIVE
Five Have a Wonderful Time

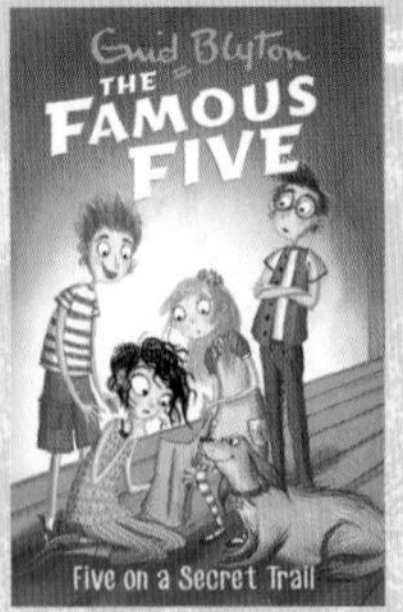
Enid Blyton
THE FAMOUS FIVE
Five on a Secret Trail

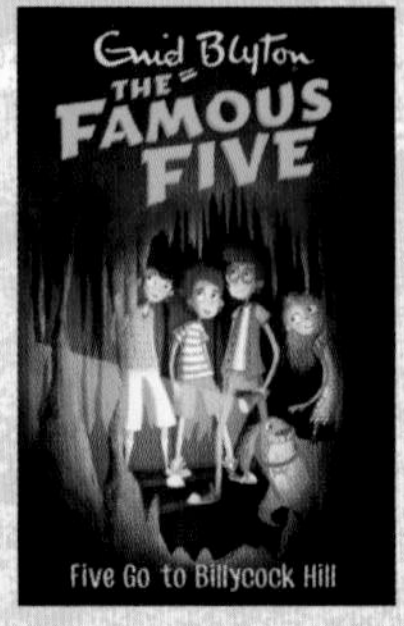
Enid Blyton
THE FAMOUS FIVE
Five Go to Billycock Hill

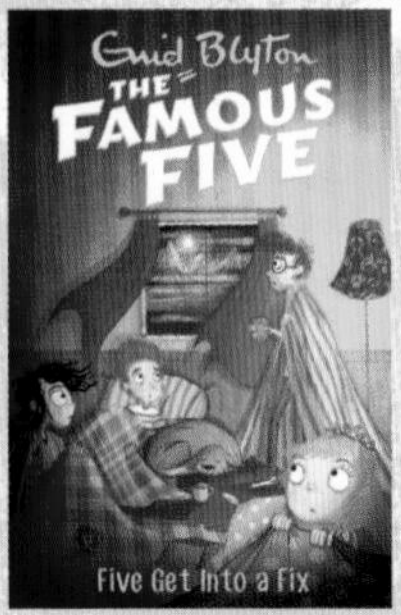
Enid Blyton
THE FAMOUS FIVE
Five Get Into a Fix

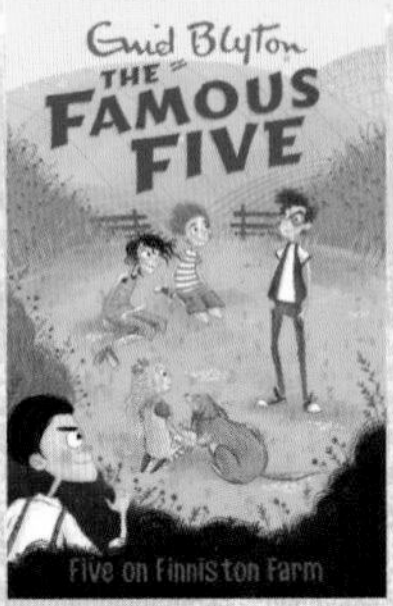
Enid Blyton
THE FAMOUS FIVE
Five on Finniston Farm

Have you read them all?

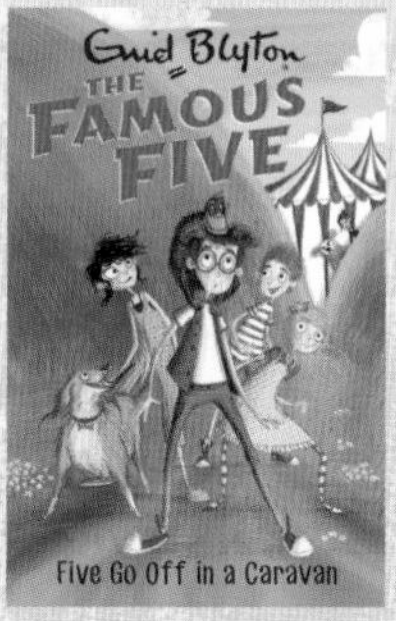
Enid Blyton
THE FAMOUS FIVE
Five Go Off in a Caravan

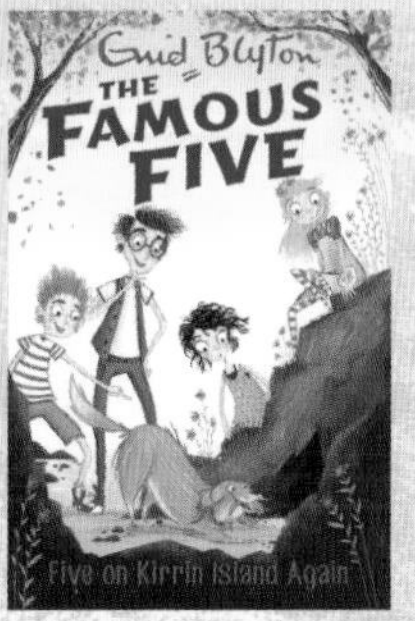
Enid Blyton
THE FAMOUS FIVE
Five on Kirrin Island Again

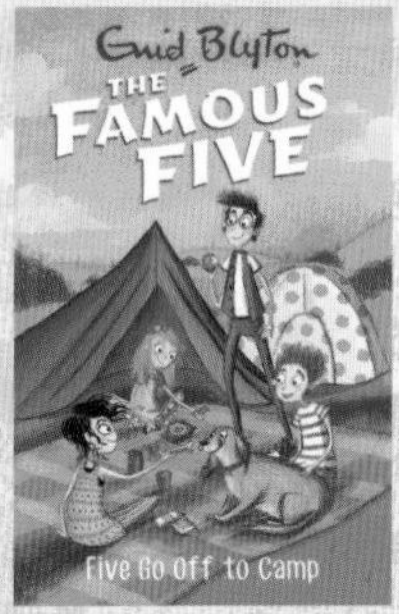
Enid Blyton
THE FAMOUS FIVE
Five Go Off to Camp

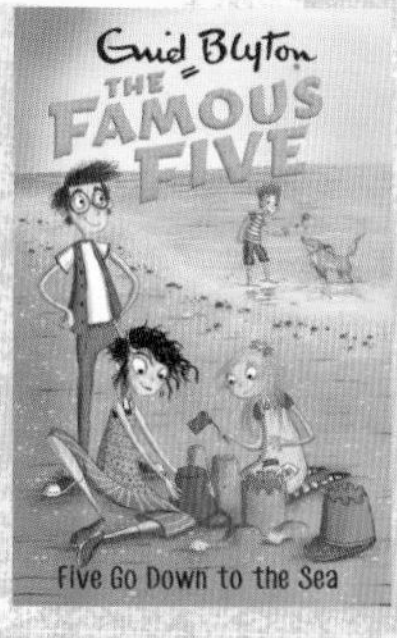
Enid Blyton
THE FAMOUS FIVE
Five Go Down to the Sea

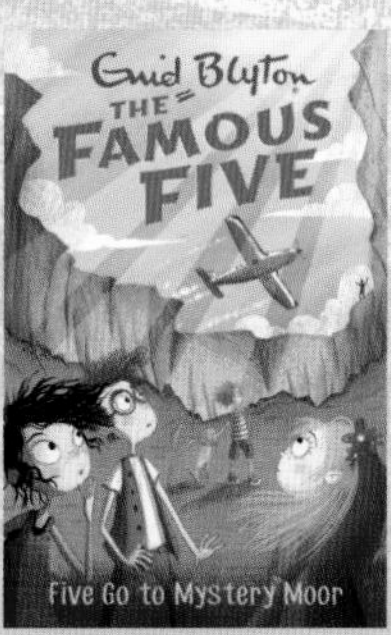
Enid Blyton
THE FAMOUS FIVE
Five Go to Mystery Moor

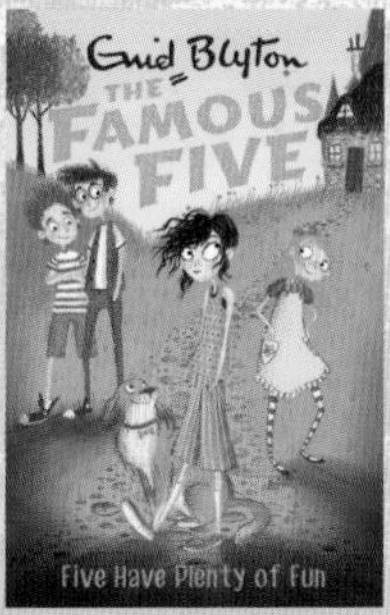
Enid Blyton
THE FAMOUS FIVE
Five Have Plenty of Fun

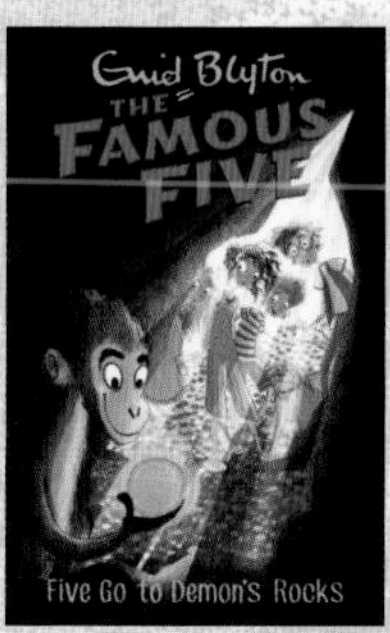
Enid Blyton
THE FAMOUS FIVE
Five Go to Demon's Rocks

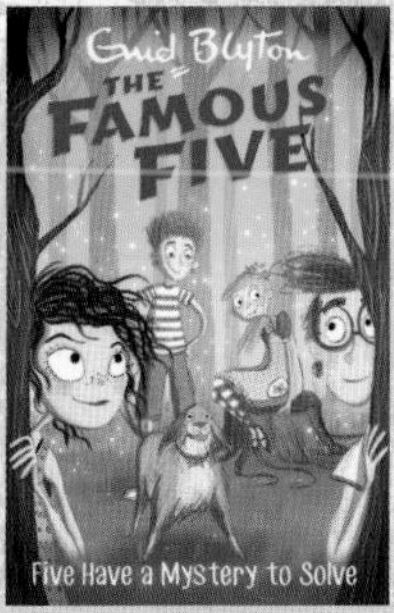
Enid Blyton
THE FAMOUS FIVE
Five Have a Mystery to Solve

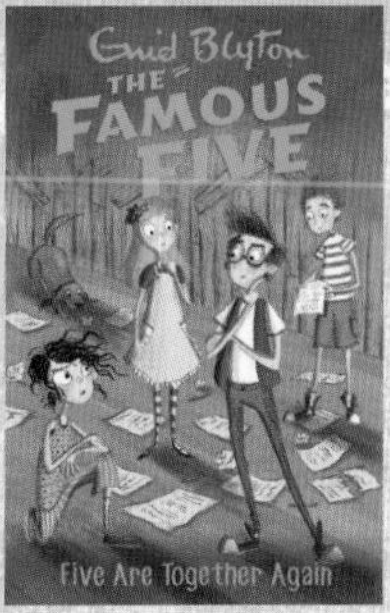
Enid Blyton
THE FAMOUS FIVE
Five Are Together Again